Praise for Marianne Wiggins and

ALMOS

"Wiggins writes stunningly polished prose and urgent, letting slip clues to both Holden's and Melanie's situations as the plot builds with a roar to the final blowout."

—*Library Journal*

"She writes with the staccato authority of an Uzi. . . . She wastes no words, thrusting scene upon scene into your face."

—*Men's Journal*

"Wiggins is a writer of substantial gifts. . . . Passion develops through hidden chains of causality, so we never know exactly where or when it's going to strike. . . . *ALMOST HEAVEN* bristles with meteorological imagery—from heat waves to hailstorms to torrential rain—all of it related to the emotional lives of her characters."

—*The New York Times Book Review*

"Wiggins is one of those critically acclaimed authors whose books acquire passionate followings . . . [like] other southern writers who find passion to be a source of both salvation and gothic nightmare."

—*Booklist*

"Wiggins unabashedly tackles the biggest themes: the vicious randomness of 'acts of God' and our attempts to grapple with them; the individual's understanding of itself and the role of memory in that construction; and the endless repetitions of history and tragedy."

—*The Washington Post Book World*

Other Books by Marianne Wiggins

Eveless Eden
Bet They'll Miss Us When We're Gone (stories)
John Dollar
Herself in Love (stories)
Separate Checks
Went South
Babe

ALMOST HEAVEN

A NOVEL

Marianne Wiggins

WSP

WASHINGTON SQUARE PRESS
PUBLISHED BY POCKET BOOKS

New York   London   Toronto   Sydney   Singapore

This book is a work of fiction. Names, characters, places and incidents are
products of the author's imagination or are used fictitiously. Any resemblance
to actual events or locales or persons, living or dead, is entirely coincidental.

 A Washington Square Press Publication of
POCKET BOOKS, a division of Simon & Schuster Inc.
1230 Avenue of the Americas, New York, NY 10020

Copyright © 1998 by Marianne Wiggins

Published by arrangement with Crown Publishers, Inc.

ISBN: 0-671-03860-5

First Washington Square Press trade paperback printing December 1999

10 9 8 7 6 5 4 3 2 1

WASHINGTON SQUARE PRESS and colophon are
registered trademarks of Simon & Schuster Inc.

Cover design by Mary Schuck; author photo by Lara Porzak

Printed in the U.S.A.

in memory of 27 August 1995

INSIDE THE CLOUD THE FUTURE STORM was staging, its raging eye caged in its fist, its potential for destruction masquerading as soft lofty brume: just another summer's afternoon in heaven.

This was weather: this is what the country was about.

Everywhere we went—New England or New York, the North, the South, the Plains states or the West—we talked about the weather. Because weather was news. For two nights in a row now, all the networks had led the evening news with bulletins about the weather: a heatwave in the South, a drought in the Midwest, a twister down in Texas.

This meant something, Holden knew. This meant something big. Something strange was going on. You can't stop feeling something strange is going on when people disappear entirely from the narrative, from news—when news starts coming at you faceless.

That's what news about the weather is, it's faceless.

It's the absence of man's fingerprint on history.

It's the advent of a new age of news where the only things worth sending crews to are encounters of the katabatic kind.

To hell with Bosnia. To hell with Kurds. To hell with Cuba when a cyclonic force is massing on the ocean off the coast of Florida and a robot in a satellite is on location, *live*.

That is our news in the millennium.

To hell with *60 Minutes* and *The New York Times*. To hell with *The Economist, Le Monde*, the Beeb, Bernstein and Woodward. Honey, they are old and cold and it is *hot* out there. And you can catch a headline on the Weather Channel any time of day.

"Dja hear about that heat they's havin in the South?" the taxi driver asks him at the airport.

"—what kinda heat?"

"—it's record breakin. Scary."

"What's so scary about heat?"

"Murder rate goes up. People lose their cool. Me, I'm prayin soon a blizzard will move in."

"In August," Holden emphasizes.

"It's a long shot," the driver shrugs. "But stranger things has happen," he's been told.

MEANWHILE AUGUST IN VIRGINIA brews daily rain.

Baking air moils upward in a mass so solid you can see it. Sometimes it sits, yellow, stinking on the James, on Ol' Jim River, like an invalid too sick to rise. Sometimes it creeps into the city, seeks its dissipation in the streets. It stares at us, the heat: it draws its bead on us and makes us plead for breeze. It smothers us in sheets. It drives us crazy.

Every evening, from the creaking porches, from the screened-in vistas of the suburbs, from the fields of brown tobacco leaf and crackling corn in Surry and in Prince George Counties, we look skyward as the day fades, and we read the

2

clouds. Without knowing we are learning how, we learn to fore-cast August thunderstorms by omens, from the signs. We learn to tell when it is coming—*rain*.

Sometimes it's the birds who give the game away, taking to the trees.

Sometimes it's a smell, the smell of copper when the sky goes green.

Sometimes it's the rhumatiz, lightnin in our bones.

People who can read it best, the best storm prophets, are the ones who navigate through thunder on their runs to heaven and they had kept his airplane on the ground. Hour had ticked by. Then another. Two. The afternoon passed. The sky above the runways had turned dark, an amber welt had risen where the sun had slipped into the Potomac. Holden had been traveling by plane for more than fifty hours and he hadn't slept. Or at least he felt as if he hadn't slept. And anyway he had no memory of it. Sleep. Do we remember sleeping?

Or do we just remember dreams.

His only recent memory was of travel. Traveling from place to place where all the places seemed the same: He had gone from Sarajevo in an armored transport two, maybe it was now three, days ago. Since then he had been moving like a mechanized target through what seemed to be a single firing range along a midway of a carnival: series of airports: Belgrade—Frankfurt—Dulles—National. At some point, too, in the last fifty hours, he had taken a taxi into D.C. and checked into the Hay-Adams. His heart, perhaps to prove that it was ticking, skipped a beat when he caught sight of his nation's Capitol, its pearly dome, in—what else?—dawn's early light. It had been morning: *shit: this* morning. Checking his watch against the local time on the Arrivals and Departures screen, he starts to realize just how well and truly fucked he is. Completely

3

hammered. No idea where he is in terms of days. " 'Scuse me," he says. He leans forward toward this fat guy in a baseball cap. The cap—black cap—has *Orioles* in fancy script across the front of it in orange. "What day is this?"

"I'm with you pal," the guy responds.

"You're *with* me . . . ?"

"If I'd drove I'd been back by now. It's the friggin weather."

"The weather, yeah. Everywhere you go. There it is. Weather."

"Wasn't always, though."

"—wasn't?"

"Nope."

"Oh, like 'in the good ol' days' . . ."

"Yep."

". . . when there wasn't any weather."

"No there was weather. Didn't stop us doin what we wanted though. When we wanted to. Didn't have these laws back then."

". . . the weather didn't."

"Back then the weather—it just was. Pure and simple. You could fly whenever you damn wanted. Go wherever. No one told you what was safe to fly or where or when to fly it. Took your life into your hands and flew. Now it's all this gov'ment regulation."

"Uh-*huh*," Holden confirms. "You got some problem with air safety?"

"Where you *from*?"

"Why?"

"Why what?"

"Why's it matter to you where I'm from?"

"Nothing. Maybe we both know someone. It's just a way of finding out."

"Like who?"

"Anybody. Someone."

"What is that, some kind of code?"

"For what?"

"I don't know—the Masons. Fellows in Christ . . . what difference does it make?"

"What are you, paranoid?"

"Absolutely. Like if I'm paranoid I'm gonna sit here and admit it. To some guy in a bird hat, even."

"Hey the Orioles ain't birds."

"And hey the Redskins ain't the first Americans . . ."

That little inner mechanism that functions as his combination shit detector/smoke alarm goes off, reminding him to check his attitude.

"So is it Sunday?" he asks. "Or have I skipped a day somewhere?"

The guy just stares at him.

"I've been traveling without a break for almost fifty hours," Holden volunteers.

"Been on the road, have you?" the guys asks real sarcastic.

"More like 'in the air.'"

"Since when?"

"Since Thursday."

"No I mean since where from?"

"From Srebrenica."

Guy grunts.

"That's in your former Yugoslavia," Holden condescends. "Don't tell me you never heard of Yugoslavia . . ."

Guy grunts again.

"Ever hear of *news*papers? Ever read one—?"

"How old are you, son—twenty-three, twenty-four? 'Cause you're an angry little shit for somebody your age."

"—twenty-*nine*, actually. And all I asked was what day it is."

"Sunday."

"—*thank* you."

"—August six. Ever heard of *that*? Dropped the goods on Hiroshima. You weren't even born."

"No. I wasn't. And frankly, that's my virtue."

"What is?"

"That I don't have to be your history lesson."

Guy leans forward on his knees and jabs a finger at him. "Oh but son, you *are* . . ."

OH, MAN: things weren't always thus.

Once upon a time he'd been this wunderkind from Brookline, Massachusetts. Only child—apple of his mother's eye, spoiled rotten to the core in Dad's opinion. Eager beaver smart-ass type, a jerk with girls. Verbal wizard, parents were the kind who *talked things through*. Things like The Environment. The Holocaust. Civil Disobedience. Our Role in Nicaragua. First kid in the neighborhood to own Nintendo. First to write a paper (after *Star Wars*) on the probable effect of computer graphics on the movie industry. First to start his own retirement fund (age twelve). First to run the Boston Marathon. First to keep a crimson banner in his junior high school locker that said "Harvard."

Yes indeedy he was going to be a millionaire by thirty: meet his Ur-Babe snowboarding in Telluride: give her that black lab in place of an engagement ring: fuck like rabbits: help her write her Ph.D. dissertation on pediatric mood disorders. Easy peasy: loft conversion in Tribeca, house on Tangier island, Chesapeake. Career in . . . ? Politics? Land and/or water rights? Venture cap?

Made no difference, really. Career was just a conduit from studenthood to tonsa-money.

So then what happened.

Something must have happened.

He'd remember in a minute.

Where do dreams go when they die?

Come to think of it there was never any weather in your former Yugoslavia. People died and people starved and people turned venous blue with cold but all the while he never noticed weather. Even though there must have been some. What the sky looked like behind the shelling. Why everybody said their legs were cold. How everybody's boots got soaked. Why everything was drenched. You just don't see specific weather when you're in a general climate. When that climate is called war. Nobody's ever gonna ask you, "Bosnia? Oh really? What's the weather like out there?"

Replacement Theory Number One:

When you're already in a killing storm, you don't need a bigger picture to inform you where the trouble lies. You don't need a satellite. You need a different life.

HELL, WHEN HE'D LEFT HARVARD eight years ago he had been master of his universe. He'd known Everything. Everything there was to know for every situation. Primed and glib and (this had been his major asset): *doubtless*. George Stephanopoulos type waaay before George Stephanopoulos. And for every George, a built-in Clinton. Built-in Bill. Built-in teacher/mentor/alter-ego.

For most of the time he was growing up, Holden's had been his dad. Everything he had done back then he did to try to please his father. Because he thought his father was the *best*, the best at everything, best at reconciling moral and political dilemmas, best at counseling the poor the sick the hungry the dispossesed, a civil saint inside the government for whom selfless civic duty was man's highest calling. Except, as is the case of many heroes, the man he was in public life was not the man he was in private.

Replacement Theory Number Two: Where one idol falls erect another.

If you can, eradicate all traces of the first.

Keep moving.

SO HE'S NOT THE FIRST SON TO DO SOMETHING STUPID OUT OF ANGER WITH HIS FATHER.

That guy's name was Adam, anyway.

Or Cain.

Sons who pull the long straws off their fathers are exceptions, not the rule.

That's what your Harvard education *doesn't* teach you: that it was ever thus. That history, as a calculus, is fixed to repetition. That men have ever taken issue with their fathers. And the world, despite the best re-imaging, isn't shaped for change. Peace is not a habit of our species. He wished his education had been different, that it hadn't led him to believe in history as a learning exercise, as a measure for improvement. History, he believed, now, with all the callow cynicism of a man in his late twenties, was not an evolution. It was a season of repeats. Been there. Done that. Ethnic cleansed at Wounded Knee; ethnic cleansed at Auschwitz. At Soweto. In Krajina. Mankind doesn't seem to profit from these massacres, Holden had come to learn. Profit morally, that is. We keep coming up with what we think are brand new reasons to extend the killing instead of saying cool your jets, here, we're too advanced for this, my daddy saw this crap in Vietnam. *His* daddy saw this crap with Hitler—et cetera, et cetera—all the way back to the first two monkeys, Cain and Abel, through a heap of daddies. Okay maybe there'd been some progress, the establishment of so-called international peace keepers, the empowerment of global cops, global tribunals: but it seemed to him it wasn't enough, it seemed to him, maybe entirely selfishly, that by the time it got to him, the progress of history should have amounted to a whole lot more.

So maybe Mister Orioles is onto something. Maybe the fat guy's right:

Four thousand years since the first Olympic Games you still can't find a person under thirty these days who knows how to put a baseball cap on straight.

It's my ponytail, isn't it? Holden asks the guy.

Guy shrugs. "If you're stupid enough to think I think your hair expresses some kinda policy position then that's your problem. Personally, my motto is? 'Free country.'"

It was the same thing with the Customs guy earlier this morning. When he told Holden to hand over the knapsack.

"You've come from where?"

"—um, you mean today?"

"What do *you* think?"

"Europe."

"Feel free to be specific."

"Frankfurt."

"And before that?"

"Your former Yugoslavia."

"And what took you over there?"

"—*what?*"

"What took you over there?"

"—um, another airplane."

"Sure. Business or pleasure?"

"It's a war zone. What do *you* think?"

"And this is—?"

"This is a modem."

"Buy it over there?"

"Well if you notice it says 'Made in the USA' right here—"

"And how long have you been gone?"

"Eight years."

"Eight *years*. And this is all you have?"

"Yes, sir."

"See your passport please?"

"How come you stopped me out of all these people? It's my ponytail, isn't it?"

"What's the nature of your trip to Washington, Mr. Garfield?"

"Is it the ponytail or not?"

"Just answer the question please."

"I'm an American, that's the nature of my trip to Washington. This is my country. Thomas Jefferson had a ponytail you know. So did George Washington. So did Ben Franklin."

"So does Dolly Parton."

"What's that supposed to mean?"

"Welcome home, Mr. Garfield."

But then again he, of all people, ought to know most things happen for no reason. Ponytail, or not the ponytail. Maybe the Customs guy was bored. Maybe his daughter has a boyfriend he can't stand with Holden's color eyes. Maybe earlier he'd told himself if some kid comes through here before eight o'clock this morning wearing faded jeans and a black linen jacket I'm gonna pull him over. Because almost everything that happens to you in your life—including love and birth and death and miracles and understanding—comes out of nowhere for no reason and scores your soul at random.

Which is how he got the job.

Same Christmas break he had the blowup with his dad—just after it, in fact. Made a call to Sydney from a Friendly's on the turnpike. Goin back to school, he said. Yeah, this early. Just nearly had to break Pooh's face.

"Your dad's? Impossible. I give it a day."

"More like give it a lifetime, Syd."

"What happened?"

"I don't wanna say."

"Given the circumstances I think you're gonna have to."

"Don't push it."

"You okay?"

"Sure I lose at least one father every day."

"Where are you?"

"Exit Seven."

"You okay to drive down here?"

"I don't wanna barge—"

11

" 'Cause otherwise Joe and I can come and get you."

"—it's Christmas. Don't wanna ruin—"

"I insist. We all insist. Come on. We're talkin 'family' here."

So next day Syd's father asked him what his plans were for the spring. After graduation.

And Holden said his plans were up for grabs.

And Syd's father asked him if he'd thought about expanding on his work at *The Harvard Crimson.*

To tell the truth, Holden told him, I don't think there's any private fortune to be made these days in journalism.

Then what are we supposed to call all this? Syd's father said.

I thought your money was inherited.

Syd's money will be, Syd's father said. Why don't you come and see me at the paper?

When Holden lists the ten men who have shaped his life—an exercise which he updates each year on New Year's Day before he's really sober—the current line-up reads like this, in increasing order of importance:

MAN	VIRTUE
Magic Johnson	grace
Alger Hiss	trust
Marcus Wineglass (Syd's father)	generosity
Vaclav Havel	style
Anwar Sadat	courage
Nelson Mandela	humility
Don DeLillo	genius
Bob Dylan	genius
Malcolm X	genius
Noah John	all of the above

The simplest things—grace, trust, humility—are the most difficult to teach. Except to the receptive, and by setting an example. Probably the hardest thing he ever had to learn was how to let the random happen. How to let it in without becoming passive. How to wait for it. How to let it happen without abdicating all responsibility for what might chance to occur. How to let life happen—not "make" it happen, *let* it. How to anticipate the random pattern. Where to place yourself to ride it safely, like a breaker, so its latent chaos doesn't toss you. Of course, not all the men whose lives he idolized had avoided the destruction in that toss. Sadat paid for his courage with his life. Hiss was a trusting fool. Malcolm wouldn't play the game by others' rules. When you watch great men in action, when you run a tape of Magic backwards, run it slo mo, when you read a paragraph of *White Noise* out loud when you're outside all alone, read every word as if you yourself are dealing and discarding from a crowded lexicon, when you watch an old clip of Malcolm speaking to a crowd in Harlem with the sound turned off, then you begin to see a common flame above them all, a spirit that unites them, like the ignition in a welder's arc. You have to look for it. You have to learn to use your eyes. You have to clock the action, stop the clock, suspend the ordinary flux of time and note right here right here right in this instant in this gesture in this lack of hesitation they let go, they do the thing no ordinary man would do and then they turn around and do it yet again each day, all of their lives, until being extraordinary becomes an ordinary habit.

His father never taught him that.

Never hauled him up in front of the TV and said Now watch the *elegance* with which this fucker moves. Never hauled him off to look at a painting, teaching him to use his eyes. Never forced him to read poetry out loud really fucking *shouting* it so he could learn to hear the skeletons in words, hear the weightless iambs rattle.

Noah did that for him—Noah John. A gift that Holden never really fathomed. Why, that is. Why a man like him, a man who had been cold to him at first, made fun of him, should suddenly change his attitude and decide to take Holden under his wing and teach him everything he knew. Random chance? Don't think so, Holden had decided. The chain of events leading to their meeting had been random, sure, each link forged by chance and not by foresight. Fight with his father. Christmas at Syd's. Job in New York for Syd's father on the paper. Then Syd's father sending him to London to train under Noah. Then the Wall. Like within a year after his arriving in London the Berlin Wall comes down, the Velvet Revolution oozes, the whole communist world decides to take a fresh look at its old men and its clapped out institutions. And Noah lets him come along. Noah shows him how to ride the chances. *God it's fabulous to be me* Holden wired Sydney from Prague on New Year's Eve, 1990.

Before he'd been to war.

Before he'd seen too many people die.

Before his friend and mentor Noah disappeared. Rode some wild high thunder till the chaos tossed him under.

Before Holden started hating what he sees in sleep.

Before he started knowing everything about his life his work his future was not so fabulous anymore.

Do you remember weather from your childhood? Can you remember a specific sky?

Two weeks ago he'd seen an infant—he couldn't tell how old, he wasn't any good in classifying babies—he'd seen a Muslim baby nailed to a tree in Serb-held territory.

Through its little arms.

14

And it seemed to be staring at the sky.

He didn't know what the baby was, at first, because of its bloat. Because of its color.

The commander of the Dutch UN unit he was following stared at the ground while two of his soldiers pried the baby off the bark with service knives. Holden could have stared at the ground, too, or at the sky or at the brilliant sunlight dancing on the treetops, but he didn't. He stood there, off to one side, and watched. At first he thought that he was watching out of habit, because observing, watching, was his job. A reporter isn't paid to blink. But even as he watched, before he'd started to compose a word about it, he knew the people that he worked for wouldn't print a piece about a Muslim baby nailed to a tree in effigy of Jesus Christ by some race-crazed Christians in some godforsaken outpost in the Balkans during July, during what was, back home, the height of baseball season. He knew whatever he might write about the baby had one chance in a million of ever seeing print on a USA news page. He knew, too, that if he wrote about the effect the incident itself, but *not the baby,* had on the innocent young blond guys from Holland, well then, hallelujah, there was a feature in the making. After all, *not the baby,* not the victim, was the media technique most journalists employed back home, wasn't it, when covering crowd-pleasing stories. What he should focus on in this particular atrocity, to get the story of this particular atrocity into print, was Not. The. Baby. The baby shouldn't be the issue. What the issue should be was the effect of war and atrocity not on those who waged war or on those who are victimized by its atrocities—but on People Like Us who merely watch. The issue was *not the baby* but whether the young Dutch guy had a baby of his own back home in Holland. Whether the young Dutch guy was wondering at this very moment how he'd

15

ever be able to lift his baby on his knee without being reminded of . . . but however much Holden tried to focus his thoughts on anything but *not the baby*, the dead baby held its ground, as if it was already a ghost.

Holden couldn't remember the last time he had touched a baby, not to mention held one, if he ever had (he supposed he must have held one at some family gathering), and here were these clean-cut Dutch kids having to try to drop this baby into a handy body bag without skin contact. Then carry it over to the truck like garbage. Not noticing the bits of baby skin and baby plasma sticking to the nails.

Isn't this what good reporters do—find the Everyman in any situation, figure out what Everyman would want to know and then deliver it? No one reading a story of this incident would ever want to think himself/herself into the part played by the *baby*, into the *baby's* skin, would they? What kind of sicko would do a thing like that?

No, people want to "see" this through the Dutch soldiers' eyes. So Holden found himself watching the two soldiers as if he was already filing the report. He watched them slip the bag over the baby like two thieves. Watched them work its body under cover of the bag and then he watched the baby's weight alter the bag's shape.

The two Dutch soldiers carried the bag between them toward the waiting UN convoy, as if they had been out together gathering ripe fruit.

"Sometimes I have to remind myself most forcefully," the Dutch commander said to Holden in his clipped and perfect English, "that we are still in Europe . . . that that infant is a *European*—do you understand?"

Sure. Just another way of saying *not the baby*, Holden thought. So he said, "Actually, that 'European' was some man and woman's child so you can go and fuck your continental self."

Maybe that's when—under *that* sky in *that* weather—it began to dawn on him he'd blown it. That he was not so fabulous, anymore. That this was no longer such a fabulous way to spend his life. And anyway: he'd lost it. He could feel it going out from under him—the balance. He was growing cautious. He wasn't sure of his ability to ride this kind of chaos anymore. Because this wasn't like it used to be when he had started. This was no Velvet movement—no revolution. This was no beginning. This was endless shit. This was stuck inside of repetition, as the ol' Bob-meister had written about a different kind of blues. And to think he could no longer remember that there had ever been a time when the only big decision of the morning had been whether or not to start the day with *Blonde on Blonde*—the two Dutch soldiers—or that other classic,
Blood
on
the
Tracks.

Acne-encrusted waldos on the Internet who never leave their rooms on the Great Plains can trade gossip with lotus blossoms in Manila these days when they want to, so imagine all the thrills in store for people who are serious news junkies. Like Holden.

He wrote one way for the magazine he worked for, and other ways for pages on the Internet.

Because the truth was he enjoyed the rank and privileges that came with working for a major US news magazine, but the mag's giant home readership was its own undoing when it came to foreign news. So online sites and chat rooms saved him. Soothed his conscience over all the money he was earning. Meant he could still respect himself. Because whatever turned to shit about this job for his former mentor Noah wasn't going to have the same effect on him. No way. He was going to find a way to handle it.

At least that's what he thought before the baby.

Still he thought he was okay that night back at the UN camp. He filed a brief report for the wire services then he went to find the two Dutch soldiers.

Both of them, for reasons that weren't clear, were under quarantine.

There was a Dutch civilian doctor attached to the Dutch unit and Holden found him sitting on a tree stump by a fence on the perimeter in the hot and moonless night, smoking.

"Is there some medical reason why those two are in separate quarantine?" Holden asked him.

The doctor looked at him, then looked awhile at the orange glow on the tip of his cigarette. "Are you Jewish?" he asked.

"Do I need to be to get this question answered?"

"You know we have in our military service not only provision for medical quarantine but also quarantine for psychological surveillance," the doctor mentioned.

"Well that's either really spooky or really enlightened," Holden said. "Like you asking if I'm Jewish."

"Because you see," the doctor said, "I think very few Christians, and probably no Jews at all, ever take the time to absorb themselves in the exercise of wondering how the process of death proceeds in crucifixion." He drew on his cigarette. "That's what I think," he announced. He stared at Holden. "I've probably seen a thousand images in my lifetime so far of Christ on the cross. How about you? Do you think that's too few? Too many? Let's say five hundred, then. That's reasonable. And still—isn't it interesting what the mind must do—I always think of that crucified Christ, that Christ that I've seen on the cross, I always think of him as having died, as the dead Christ. I have to make myself remember that he was alive for most of the time he was there. He died there, yes. But he was alive for most of the time. Alive when they drove in the nails. Do you see what I'm saying? Those nails through the skin. Through the tissue of Him. But I'm not talking about the religious significance of Christ on the cross." The doctor paused, then continued. "No. I'm talking about those boys, aren't I? That's what you asked me. Why they're in quarantine. Because sooner or later, if not already, they're going to realize that that baby wasn't dead when it was nailed to that tree."

He stood, tamped his cigarette into the dirt, and disappeared among the shadows.

Ten days later, after air reconnaissance flights had spotted them, Holden was one of the first people on the ground to find the mass graves at Srebrenica. Six thousand—maybe eight thousand—dead. Eight thousand. Men. And boys. Like a dump site. Like those pictures of extermination camps in World War II. Tangle of human remains. Most of them buried alive.

And that was it, really.

For him.

End of the ride.

Fun while it lasted:

He crashed.

THEY CALL IT the flashbulb effect.

Next thing he knew he was in the Frankfurt airport calling his desk back in the States.

"So hey you want to get somebody in there pretty quick," he heard himself explaining, " 'cause this is gonna be the biggest story to come outta there since—"

"Yeah. We know. You're not exactly waitress of the week this week. What were you, shot in the head or something? Some people around here thought you might be dead but then I reminded them guys like you don't die before sending in their own obituaries."

"—'guys like me'?" Holden looked through the glass partition of the phone booth at the crowd milling through the airport. "Do I know you?"

"No."

"—so where do you get off saying shit like that about me?"

"—where do *I* get off? Me? I'm the person who stayed up all night two nights in a row to file those Missing In Action reports about you, that's who I am. One with State and one with UNPROFOR. If you've never had to deal with that you ought to try it sometime. Lodsa fun."

"So you want a 'Thank You' note?"

"No I want you to remember next time you need to take a crap do it in your own stream not in mine."

Holden closed his eyes. And there it was. Flashbulb effect on the inside of his eyelids. Landscape he could not identify where the sky was green and the ground was bathed in orange.

He put the phone down and slung his knapsack on his shoulder. He had nothing with him but his laptop and this knapsack full of rough essentials. In his wallet he had leftover paper money from a dozen countries and some credit cards he hadn't used the whole time he'd been in Bosnia. Six months. Still a war zone that wasn't taking Visa.

So he was, like, max in credit.

Going anywhere he wanted was not a fiscal problem. Anywhere his passport would allow. His passport—the one with that rampant eagle clutching weapons in one claw, an olive branch gripped in the other stamped on the front. In gold. Open sesame, it said. Speak my language walk my walk I'm coming through, *American* the beautiful. He could even understand why it's still called flashbulb, even though flashbulbs are pretty much antique.

It's a protein thing.

Memory is.

The way it works, way it leaves its fingerprints, way the brain encodes it: indiscriminately. It's been proven we remember better when we're feeling strong emotions. Like pictures snapped in bright light, bright conditions, extra vivid, coded neuronally with the added ooomph of anger horror fear despair or hope. Or love. Always go for love. Pray you've saved those memories of love.

He was standing in the Frankfurt airport in this kind of über-newsstand place, long long rows of magazines and papers floor to ceiling from around the world, German papers in the forefront, DIE WELT DIE ZEIT *Frankfurter Allgemeine Zeitung für Deutschland,* then the French, Italian, Spanish, Arabic, Scandinavian, Greek, Czech, English, Irish, Scottish, Asian—news from everywhere, from journalists like himself from every print producing outpost on the planet, hall of mirrors that's what this place was, except every image it repeated was a different slant a different take a different shape a different picture. Row after row—*Vogue* in seven languages, *Marie-Claire* in five, all the French ones in a line next to the Italian, all the English, all the Spanish, then a shelf of vivid bright familiars like a

21

display of Campbell soup cans. *Vanity Fair. GQ. Mirabella. House &
Garden. Scientific American. Psychology Today.* He hadn't seen some
of these in months or even longer. *Harper's. Time. U.S. News &
World Report. Newsweek's* banner, white on black, read HIROSHIMA
AUGUST 6, 1945 over the red and white teaser superimposed on a vin-
tage picture of the mushroom cloud proclaiming, WHY WE DID IT,
and suddenly the whole place seemed to take a power surge as if a
flash had gone off, and his hands began to shake, yes yes *yes* he was
excited to know WHY, he wanted to know why "we" "they" "anybody" did it, does it, and his vision blurred the decorated sets,
celebs, porn models, cheesecake tits and ass—the bomb—swam
together in an explosion of bright light and he recorded in that
instant longing so profound it made him weep:

He wanted to go home.

YOUR NATION DOESN'T MISS YOU when you're gone.
Your nation doesn't send a scout to search for you or pine your
absence pacing on its shores: it keeps the door unlocked and soldiers on.

When the cabdriver asked him where he was going, Holden
gave the name of the first hotel in D.C. that came to mind, a
classy joint that didn't usually get unexpected guests showing up
at dawn, looking pretty shaky yet strangely enigmatic.

Or so the perky woman at Reception thinks.

He seems vaguely American to her yet somehow European.
No doubt it's the heady mixture of his Italian linen jacket (very
rumpled), chocolate eyes, faded black Lacoste tennis shirt (missing all its buttons), cute buns, loafers with no socks, ponytail and
Gold Card.

Definitely not your average lobbyist.

Maybe in the entertainment business.

Maybe in from California.

"The only thing I have available for immediate occupancy, Mr. Garfield, is an executive suite."

"Fine."

"—but I can put you in a queen-size double with a meal plan later."

"I'll take the suite," Holden says, noticing her teeth.

"Well I can offer you a corporate rate with that if you're staying longer than two nights."

"Great," Holden says.

Funny, things you notice when you've been away.

You know you've been away too long when you start noticing the teeth of women from your own tribe:

Her teeth are huge.

"And how many keys will you be needing?"

"Well how many locks are there?" he says.

She looks confused.

"Sorry," he says. "Just one. You, ah . . . you've got," he mentions as she gives the key card to a bellboy, "really nice teeth."

"Oh thanks," she twinkles. "I floss."

"You see?" Holden says, smiling, leaning toward her across the desk. "People in Europe don't let you in on details like that."

"Oh are you from Europe?"

She's smiling broadly.

Is it our diet? Is there fluoride in the air?

"Massachusetts," Holden volunteers.

"Oh we have a Massachusetts Avenue here!"

Holden blinks.

"What would you have said if instead I'd said I'm from Alaska?"

the size of things

"I would have said I *knew* you were West Coast . . ."

Holden knows it will wear off soon enough, this sense he is a stranger in a strange land. Still he thinks it is terrific when the bellboy palms his tip and says muchas gracias, en*joy*.

It was the size of things. And not just teeth. Size of personal space. Size of the TVs. (His suite had three.) The abundance, size of personal selection. As if a choice of only two things signals poverty. Everything looked slightly pumped. Steroid enhanced wallpaper. Vitamin enriched views. Do Not Disturb in stereo.

He knows this first take of his will eventually prove wrong. Not wrong in the sense that it is not true—it *is* true: he is in a set of giant rooms—but wrong in the sense that while this version of America is true it isn't true enough. He'd been away eight years, long enough to have heard more generalizations about America and Americans than he once thought could have existed. So he knows no single statement about America and 'mericans ever really nails it, never leaves him breathless, thinking finally right yes that's it that's us that's me that's who I am. Of every truism or truth you think you've learned about America its half-truth is just as accurate. But so's its other half. So's its opposite. Our herding instinct drives us into the group therapy of group I.D. but then every bit of masticated pap we've fed on from day one about the do-able, about dream fulfillment and the pursuit of happiness, fires up those engines of rebellion that drive each and every one of us apart, toward individualism. Here we are: herd of potential presidents. Rabble of wannabes, every one of us a lion king. Every one of us an as-yet-undiscovered star. A culture of eventual cult leaders. Everything you've heard or seen or read or thought about this place and we its people is absolutely true. And false. Only place on earth actively seeking to divide itself, to hyphenate itself in order to define the whole. That's why foreigners can never

24

understand us. Never get our history, grasp our Civil War, for example, never really come to grips with it as being more significant in understanding our national identity than even, say, the war for independence or the monster land grab West or the invention of the repeating rifle.

Because if history teaches anything about we the people it's that Americans are leavers.

Seceding from the Union, going into space or leaving Saigon, we're outta here, we're vacating these premises even as we're pledging allegiance to the flag and promising to stay. Because one way or another someday, if not already, all of us will have left some one some where some dream some loneliness some thing. And split. Disconnected our phones. Hyphenated our habituation and hotfooted out of town. For a better life than this one, see? For the pursuit of. Why else are we so fascinated with what the weather's doing down in Texas while we're watching our TVs in the District of Columbia unless we're looking for a break between disasters?

So we can start to pack.

IT MUST COST ALMOST NOTHING to produce, he thinks. The way they'd set it up—it's fascinating. Took the proven CNN format of low presenter numbers, then slashed it. What did they have—six, maybe ten in-front-of-camera bodies? Each one a specialist. Like this gust guy. Second time in fifteen minutes he's been on live talking about gusting. In between: the high-low lady. Only highs and lows. No gusting. That's the gust guy's job. Then six times an hour they do this thing called "On the Eights." Eight after, eighteen after, twenty-eight after, thirty-eight after, forty-eight after, fifty-eight, they go to local. That's the genius part. Six

25

times an hour for a minute every time—six minutes every hour—
they put the local weather on the screen so you can read it. Really
local, like a five-mile radius from where you're watching. Has to
cost them nothing. Like some pittance of a license fee to down-
load data from the National Weather Service. Practically automatic. Virtually non human.

Even the music.

That's the bit that's fascinating. While the data's up, the
Eights, while that's on the screen—highs, lows, what it's doing
now, right now at this instant—they play music.

Wouldn't you just love that job?

Be the Weather Channel d.j.

What a trip.

Holden would love that job. Bring real genius to it. Do it with
panache, not just toss the opp away the way they did it now—what
was this junk that they were playing now? Ravel's *Bolero*? What
does Ravel's *Bolero* have to do with weather? No man, what he'd
do is sync the music to the forecast. Have at hand your Sunshine
tracks. Your Rainies. All your Stormy songs. Really make a decent
set of it. Throw in Handel's *Water Music* during dry spells for a
laugh. Mess with people's heads. Play Dylan's "Hurricane" to see
if any calls come in to say hey that song's about a person. Not a
storm front. Not a pressure system. A real person.

Holden's standing watching the TV screen with the remote
in one hand, Bloody Mary in the other. He had ordered up this
huge swank breakfast, dumped the entire contents of his knapsack
on the floor and sent every piece of clothing he had with him to
be washed. Like what the lady who turned up to collect it called
a first class laundering. First time for months. Then he'd taken a
thirty-minute first class laundering himself. Long hot shower.
Then the breakfast came. Still too early in the morning to really

think about activities so he mixed the Bloody Mary at his bar and walked around the hotel suite in a hotel robe switching on the three TVs. Thinking maybe all these rooms wasn't such a fabulous idea. Because he couldn't fill them. No gaiety no strength of purpose no possessions. No direction. No friends and family. No honey to come home to. Three TVs for consolation. Choice of fifty channels. He's standing in the middle of the room too antsy to sit down and eat. Surfing. Weather Channel. CNN. C-SPAN. (Who's this? Wait. Oh: Janet Reno.) Cartoons. Waco hearings. Weather Channel. Porn. Spanish station. Lifestyle Channel. Waco hearings. Weather. Porn. Woman fondling her nipples. Woman's breasts taking up the screen, her fingernails are sharp and long. Larger than life size. Dangerous around her nipples. Holden turns the sound off. Nipples extra long, too, and erect. Like nipples on those baby bottles. Holden puts the drink down and walks over to the screen. He puts both hands on top of the TV, looks down and watches his cock rub back and forth between those tits. All through high school and college, with or without visual stimulus, he'd never had a problem with this stuff. In the shower—in his car. At his desk. Wherever. He used masturbation so as never to have to use a woman purely for sex. Over the years, through his brief life as a man, he'd come to believe he had two different sex lives, one that was private, that was his alone—and one that was public, with somebody else. Sometimes the two intersected, more often they didn't, and that was just fine. By himself he could always come off like a hero. On his own, at least one of his sex lives had always been active. And failproof. Fulfilling. Look ma, no hands.

And no prob.

Until now. He would start, like now with the TV—something would start it, that urge to make sex. And he'd start to do

27

what he knew how to do from so many years of pleasurable practice but then little by little over the past several months this problem developed. Snag in the shag. Something else would kick in. A self-conscious thought. A shit-laden memory. It was war—he knew that. Knew, too, war exacted a price from the civvies, higher price from civilians than from the pros. Soldiers are trained how to fight and then fuck. How to see death, then forget. Go from death mutilation and shit back to fucking. Back to the "L" word. Back to tender communion. "What do you guys, ah, do about sex?" he'd asked some French soldiers one night bivouacked near Banja Luka. He figured if any foreign legion would have a help line for fucking the French would, *Mais non.* She stays at home, the sex, they told Holden. Soldiers are priests. Where there's violence then they must forget about sex. Because the two do not belong together. But he didn't know how to stop longing for love. He'd never been the kind of man like his father who put on a persona each working day in the form of a suit and then took it off on the weekend and put on another. The kind of man who compartmentalized his life into categorical lots. One way of being with women, one way of being with men. One way for watching the killing. One way for watching her breasts. They don't make bulletproof vests for the psyche, or do they? Maybe that's what it is, a man's machismo. A kind of man's costume. A set of disguises. A shield. Maybe being a man means dressing in manhood. Strapping it on. Maybe being a man is first learning what love is—how to love—and then forcing yourself to forget love exists.

Plenty of men who do that, right?

Plenty.

Right?

Who would never be caught with their cocks in their fists standing alone in a goddamn hotel room in front of a televised

28

naked woman crying his fucking guts out to be loved like some kinda baby.

At eight-thirty that morning he found himself sitting on the bed with one of those little bottles of Smirnoff from the bar in his hand, staring at the entry for his father in the District of Columbia phone book. He was going after Sydney's number and the book went open in the Gs and then he got up and poured another of those little Smirnoffs from the bar into his empty glass and sat down again and read down the column to his father's name and number. House in Georgetown. Bastard.

Took a swallow off the vodka and went ahead and looked up Sydney. On Columbia Road? Funky. It was ridiculously early, but. What are best friends for. A woman answers.

"Ah, hi," Holden says. "Speak to Sydney, please?"

"O—my—gawd!"

"Ah . . . wait. I might have the wrong— Is Sydney there?"

"This *is* Sydney, Holden!"

Whoa, he thinks.

"—this is so weird! We were just talking about you last night when we were talking about the guest list and Sydney said you'd never make it for the wedding because you'd still be out in Bosnia . . ."

Whoa, *whoa*. Penny drops.

"—*Syd*ney? This you?"

"—well, who the hell did you think you were calling?"

"I thought I was calling the other— Forget it. So how *are* you? What are you doing at Syd's place?"

"I live here."

"You live at Syd's."

"Well of course I do."

Silence.

"—Holden?"

". . . sorry. I'm. Jet lag. You know. What wedding?"

"Sydney's and mine."

Silence again.

"—Holden?"

". . . sorry."

"Next month."

"You and Syd."

"—are getting married."

"You and Syd are."

"Next month."

"—and you don't think that's just a bit too coincidental?"

"—why, are you getting married, too?"

"The bride and groom both named Sydney."

"—isn't it cute?"

"—and the groom being my best friend from college and the bride being my girlfriend from college."

"Well Holden," she says in that way he remembers she always had, "our getting married isn't about you. Start again?"

"—hi, Syd."

"Hi, Piglet."

"Please don't call me Piglet—"

"—so are you back? Where are you calling from, you sound so close—"

"—I'm back for a while, yeah. I'm not really sure yet, I just got into town."

"O my gawd, when can we see you? Hey, bummer about Pooh and Kanga, I'm like so totally sorry for you, Pig. The bastard. How's Kanga holding up? I took her to lunch soon as I heard, she tell you?"

"You took my mother to lunch?"

"Soon as I heard. I figured, this town? So-called friends will drop her to follow Pooh. This town always follows power."

"Well that was . . . white of you Sydney."

"I think it backfired though."

"—what do you mean?"

"I don't think she had such a great time seeing me. The opposite, in fact."

"Why do you say that?"

"Well it was dumb of me not to tell her in advance about the implants and she kept staring at them. Like thinking oh. So that's what twenty-nine-year-olds look like these days. You know. Not seeing them as me. Seeing them as part of whatzername new Mrs. Pooh."

"—'implants'?"

"So now like I make a point of telling everyone from my former life about them. Like you. So it doesn't come as such a shock."

"What implants?"

"Oh we're C cup now."

"What were we before?"

"—doesn't Pig remember?"

A question you can only answer yes to even if you don't.

He glances over at the TV screen.

"Well, well," he says. He clears his throat. "Congratulations all around then Sydney."

LET ME GET THIS STRAIGHT:

"You're actually going to marry her?"

"I actually am."

"Whose idea was this?"

"You mean who asked who?"

"Yeah."

"Sydney asked Sydney."

"—why?"

"—bells rang. Alarms went off. I don't know, Marcus dying and all that . . ."

"Oh hey you know how I felt about that. I was really sorry not to be there for you, bro. You know how much your dad meant to me . . ."

"—yeah, well. Sorry about Pooh and Kanga."

"—no comparison."

". . . and well listen: Sydney's not the girl we knew in college."

"—obviously *not*."

"She's a different woman now—oh. Did she mention—"

"—they came up. Yes. She mentioned them. —so what's the deal there? You're the Editor?"

"I take it you haven't been checking your e-mail?"

"Not for a while, no. Not for like. Months."

"Tina Brown came through and raided our talent for *The New Yorker*. Bottom line: there was a vacuum. I filled it."

"In other words she didn't offer you a job."

"In other words she didn't."

"So in other words if I need a job—"

"—do you?"

"—I should call Tina."

"—Holden? —you serious? What's going on?"

"I'm . . . don't know. Need to talk to you."

"Sure. Absolutely. Let me finish up this piece and I can come to your hotel in, say, an hour—?"

"I need to get out Syd—"

"Fine come here then."

"—no I mean out out."

"—'out' out. Like what. Like kill the goose what lays the—"

"I pay a price for all that money, shit. You're the one behind the desk . . ."

"Is this why Boot is looking for you?"

"Boot—?"

"—you didn't get my e-mail about Boot?"

"—when?"

"—'cause he kept calling like five times. Boot. About a month ago asking me if I knew if you knew where Noah is. Something about a sister."

"—about a nun?"

"—no Noah's sister. Does Noah have a sister? —Holden? You listening to me?"

A memory stirs—a picture of a woman.

"Syd, I'll call you back," he mentions, hanging up.

Like an involuntary reflex, he dials Boot's number and there's Boot's voice, the ghost called forth, announcing, *Boot, here* like it's an army barracks instead of his summer house out in the Hamptons.

"I hear you're looking for me," Holden says.

"—well well well. Hotshit little smart ass. If it isn't. I was betting you thought you're too famous these days to talk to me. Even though I'm the one what made you."

"What do you want Boot."

"Noah. John."

"—no clue."

"—it's not what you think."

"You don't know what I think."

"Let me spell it: John has a sister. Ring any bells? Married. Four kids. Living somewhere near Richmond. Virginia. Melanie. Married name Page. Five weeks ago this woman sees her four kids and husband killed. All of them. Witnesses it. So now this doctor down there in the loony bin at Medical College of Virginia needs a living relative. Because this woman's in his ward with total memory loss. Hysterical amnesia. *Told* you this wasn't what you thought it was."

"Doctor's name—?"

"Graham. Alexander Graham."

"Where's this Medical College of—?"

"Richmond."

"—so now the only question is do I say thank you Boot or just goodbye?"

Sydney had always been the better writer of the two of them, but Holden was the better bloodhound. Holden was a digger. Noah had taught him how, up to a point, but you either have the blooding instinct or you don't. And Holden had it. Sydney didn't. Which you sometimes didn't notice because Sydney's writing is so good. Until afterward when you tried to remember what the hell you'd learned. If anything. Whereas Holden is a fact man, plain and simple. Not a stylist. With him either there are facts or there's no story. And he can always get the facts that make a story. Always.

This one any average idiot could do.

Bell Atlantic gives him residence and office phones for a Dr. Alexander Graham. Both in Richmond. Also tells him Graham's specialty is neuropsychiatry. Also gives the main number for Medical College of Virginia.

Which gives him the psychiatric ward.

Which won't give out patient information but confirms that Dr. Alexander Graham is attached to the psychiatric unit. Is it urgent? Yes? Well can you hold? Dr. Graham is in fact at this very moment with us on the floor.

Two minutes later a courtly Southern accent in a Southern Comfort voice announces, Dr. Graham here-ah.

"—Dr. Graham my name is Holden Garfield and I'm a friend of Noah John's."

"—well am I happy to hear from you!"

"I hope so, sir, because I want to try and be as much help in this matter as I can and I don't know how much you've been told about my friend's current situation but, um, I was wondering if I could possibly meet with you sometime soon to—"

"—how 'bout tomorrow mornin?"

"That would be ideal, sir."

"—can you make it round this time?"

"—yes."

"—say ten o'clock?"

"Fine by me."

"—you just come on up to the fourth floor here. We're in North Buildin. Fourth floor. You just ask for me at the nurses' station when you get here. No one gets past my nurses, any way . . ."

SO FOR THE FOURTH TIME IN TWO DAYS he's in another airport. Waiting for another plane.

Amnesia—shit there's a concept. Could use a bit of that myself. Forgiveness and forgetness, right there in the dictionary next to *amnesty*. Same root word. Meaning "not remembered."

But something "not remembered" is not the same as something's that forgotten.

Two different concepts.

The two different halves of truth and reconciliation.

Because your mind can consciously exile a memory. Pretend to forget.

But your mind can't reconstruct what is truly lost.

Amnesia is the selective loss of access to specific memory data that have emotional significance.

Some amnesias result from trauma to the fabric of the skull. Some are transitory, brief confusions passing like swift clouds over the landscape of the conscious mind after epileptic seizures. Like weathers. Like a twister. After a blow to the head. After a shock.

Some stop the clocks entirely.

Freud called these amnesias defense mechanisms. Replacing, in the mind, the hands of time with the mechanics of hysteria.

In hysterical amnesia the self, that organ of remembering, opens its veins and bleeds itself to death.

Think of a body drowning in self-generated fluid.

To the mind that's what amnesia is.

A self-inflicted death.

In order to survive.

The conscious mind can't induce forgetfulness except by way of mind-altering substances, but the unconscious mind can and does. The unconscious mind is always ticking, ever tidal, never tidy. A dark sea through which shifting floes of pale remembrances loom and groan, wordlessly, like ice.

Memory is all we are and all we have. A re-construction of the past. Not its reproduction.

Something like a gallows or a birdcage that the mind constructs.

It is the monument we build inside ourselves.

Each soul constructs its own.

And it is either everything we've kept in life. Or everything we've lost.

How it works and what it means is one of those lasting—if not the only—mysteries of life. How our memories play tricks on us, as if they are not part of us. How memories haunt. How they recur in vivid living color.

A photograph he hadn't seen in years.

Average photo album family portrait, color snapshot, five by seven, framed on Noah's desk in London. Man and woman on a beach. With kids. Everyone in bathing suits. Woman in a black bikini.

What are you staring at? Noah had said.

She was honey colored in the picture, honey-colored hair fanning out behind her in the wind. One of that type of blonde you dream about if you're going to dream of blondes. Who have the impossible combination of being very long and very slender with a ballerina's legs and barmaid's breasts.

But there was something else.

Low on her abdomen just above the bikini line.

Holden had picked the photo up to get a better look.

"Melanie," Noah had said. "My sister and her family."

"How old is she?"

"Mel? When this was taken? Thirty-eight, thirty-nine . . ."

"Jesus what a body."

"My *sister's?*"

That's what Holden remembers.

Noah looking at him like he was a pervert.

And her pearly scar.

That delicious Mona Lisa smile slung like a satin rope across her pelvis just below her navel.

ALL RIGHT PEOPLE, LISTEN UP the co-pilot says. "We've got some serious weather in front of us."

He is a young guy, a few years older than Holden—tan, a body builder who looks too big for both this toy plane and his short-sleeved shirt with its toy epaulets.

"There's a storm system out there," he says as if they hadn't noticed. "Now we can stay clear of it pretty well by running parallel to it down to Richmond. But as for the second leg to Newport News—how many of you want to go to Newport News?"

The blue-haired lady in the seat in front of Holden turns to look around the cabin.

It's early evening and most of the original passengers on this flight had gone back into D.C. hours ago to wait the storm out or had gone on by other routes.

Like the guy in the Orioles baseball cap keeps mentioning, if they'da driven they'da been where they was going to by now.

Which was certainly true.

You can drive from D.C. to Richmond in two hours—but for now, when they line up to go out to the little Cub on the runway, there are seven of them left. The pilot and the co-. Holden. This ancient blue-hair relic with a parasol and white gloves in the seat in front of him. Pair of salesmen at the back. And across the aisle from him, the guy in the Orioles baseball cap.

"Raise your hands all of you who want to try for Newport News," the co-pilot is saying.

"—excuse me?" Holden says. "—you want us to *vote?*"

"Okay three for Newport News," the co-pilot says.

"Don't you love this country?" Orioles asks Holden.

He is one of the majority.

"—I just love this country!" he repeats.

It was like the hundredth time he's said it. Like you could run any inanity past him it would evoke this spontaneous love.

"Let's get this baby off the ground," the co-pilot is saying. "You all right there, ma'am?" he asks the blue hair.

She is having trouble sitting still.

"I don't want to go through any thundercloud," she tells him.

"No, ma'am," he assures her, "we'll make sure you don't."

The cabin lights go off and the props begin to roar.

Blue hair turns around and peers at Holden. Her face looks like a turkey's coming round the seat. "My mister once got caught inside a thundercloud in France during the war!" she shouts over the din. "Tore his parachute to pieces—left him deaf, God bless him!"

The little plane begins to taxi.

From his window Holden sees the storm flank over the Potomac like a phantom country.

Like the blue hair's husband, Kanga's dad, his grandfather, had been a paratrooper in World War II and Holden reckoned if he were still alive he'd be about as old as this old lady. He worked for General Electric and spent a good part of his life jumping out of airplanes into thunderstorms and making miniature blizzards with dry ice in the home freezer. Guy was nuts, Holden now considers—but the kind of nut who's tons of fun for any kid to have for a grandfather. F.X. the old man's name was—and as they lift off the ground Holden wonders if there's any place on earth other than America where people go through their entire lives being called by their initials. Anyway—what a kick—F.X. doesn't automatically stand for Francis Xavier these days. If the old guy had lived long enough he could have watched his initials evolve from the name of a saint into a special effect. Or maybe a saint *is* a special effect, Holden thinks. At any rate F.X. would have *loved* this one.

"—wouldcha look at *that*—!" Orioles is shouting.

He's leaning way into the aisle to get a better look from Holden's side.

Beethoven's brain, Holden marvels.

What the storm looks like in the dark. Inside the clouds. Booming and switching.

On and then off.

Symphonic explosions, but mute.

Like Beethoven composing.

Sixteen million thunderstorms like this one a year—he knew that from F.X. Sixteen mill on the surface, not counting the ones that occur higher up in the atmosphere.

That's forty-five thousand a day.

Just under two thousand an hour.

How memory works: why is he thinking of this?

Try to track memory back:

And of course that would lead him to F.X. because he was a paratrooper, too.

But how many times had Holden seen lightning in the sky from a plane? Ten times? Maybe twenty? Even now as he watched this storm rumble and rage he remembers a day years ago, twenty years ago, when Padge—his nickname for F.X.—took him to the

40

Science Museum in Boston to see lightning made. There was this big Frankenstein thing in this circular room. The Van de Graaf. Big thing that made bolts of lightning snap from it to the ceiling. Scariest motherest thing in the world—Holden had felt the zap of its ions discharge in his heart. Padge had loved it. "Fifty thousand degrees Fahrenheit, son," he told Holden, "five times hotter than the roasting you'd get on the sun. Traveling four hundred twenty million feet per second. Striking one hundred times every second around the circumference of the earth. Discharging four billion kilowatts every second, each day . . ."

"—but will *ya look at that?*" Orioles is still shouting.

Holden senses he is starting for his side of the plane when, suddenly, he feels a charge up his legs.

Tingling on his thighs.

Old lady's hair in front of him fanning out like blue aura. When she reaches up to feel it's still there sparks fly off her white fingers.

There is a fizz like poured seltzer.

An orb of light appears from the cockpit two feet off the floor.

Stalls there, fizzing, for a fraction of a second before setting a course straight down the aisle.

But Orioles is on his feet, standing in its path, caught there, transfixed like proverbial deadmeat by headlights as the ball of lightning speeds at him, sizzles up his front and down his back before it zips on down the aisle and disappears with an enormous bang into its element, the air.

Suddenly there's a stink of burn and panic.

Orioles is prostrate in the aisle, rigid as a lightning rod and dead for all Holden knows until he rips his shirt open and starts doing what he hopes is CPR.

Twenty minutes later they're on the ground in Richmond in the humid twilight.

41

An ambulance is waiting on the runway.

"Cardiac?" the ambulance driver asks Holden.

She's a large wide woman in a white uniform with a name tag on her chest that reads *Ezola*.

"—guess so," Holden murmurs.

He's looking at the ambulance.

"Still breathin?"

"Yep."

The ambulance has MEDICAL COLLEGE OF VIRGINIA painted on the side of it.

"Where you takin him?" Holden asks.

"Well if he ain't dead we'll take him into MCV. That's where we're from."

Holden lifts his knapsack to his shoulder.

"Mind if I hitch a ride with you?"

"You a relative?"

In the past he might have played the lie to nail the story but now he digs into his pocket and pulls out a ruined press pass. "No," he says. He tries to look as if he still believes it. "I'm a reporter."

Sure wisht that storm had come through here, Ezola's saying as she tears toward Richmond, siren shrieking. "My tomatoes are real pooped. Plus every day this heat gives us another cardiac. But people havin heart attacks on planes, I'll tell ya. If I had a heart condition I wouldn't *drive*, much less go twenty thousand feet up in the air."

"He didn't have a heart attack," Holden says, keeping a hand on the dashboard to help him get used to her speed.

"He was struck by lightning," he tells her.

"—*no.*"

"—yeah. Ball lightning."

"Whatcha mean by ball?"

"—shaped like a ball."

"How big?"

"—like a basketball."

"Inside an airplane?"

Holden nods.

Ahead of them he starts to see the lights atop the city.

"I had an uncle onest was struck by lightning out in a tobacco field," she says. "Standin there this bolt comes down, next thing we know his clothes is ash and he's walkin 'round without a memory."

"—amnesia?"

"No idea who is who or what was what. Well, it figures, doesn't it. We use that electric shock on violent patients. Calm 'em down and empty out their brains. And that's what lightning is, electric shock. And it's what makes the brain work anyway, you think about it. E-lectricity."

Holden's looking at the skyline.

"So what is there to do in this town?"

"—this town? Son, Richmond is the capital of the South! I've lived in Richmond all my life and I ain't never been bored with it but onest or twice. We got baseball! We got the stock cars! Jazz! You just missed the jazz festival was here last week."

"What about a good hotel?"

"You got money? 'Cause you got money, then the best hotel be Hotel Jefferson. *Every*body stay the Jefferson. Tom Cruise. That 'Pretty Woman.'"

"—near the hospital?"

"Not near enough, but this city has taxi drivers. Why you ask? You reportin somethin about MCV? —yeah? Because if you are let me tell you you won't find a better teachin hospital anywhere in the United States. I should know. I borne my children there and I been working there these past twenty years."

"—so you think it's good."

"I do!"

"What's so good about it?"

"People's attitude—I mean it's Virginia, isn't it? You stay 'round here a while you'll see. People is real nice down here."

"—why do you say 'down' here?"

"Well it's obvious you're from up North."

"—why's it obvious?"

"Well for one thing you ask a lot of questions. And another you ain't volunteered a thing about you self except to git the ride off me."

"Maybe I'm shy."

"—you ain't shy, you just uptight."

She pulls off the highway onto an exit ramp toward what appears to be the center of the city.

"This here is Broad. All these buildings here? The hospital. Down there? The river. Head down toward the river six blocks you come to Shockoe Slip. That's what you want. Good hotels— the Berkeley and the Omni. Good restaurants. Plenty places with good music. Shops an' all. What you look for is East Cary Street. Easy walking distance. You stay at Richmond Omni you look my son up, he works there, he'll treat you right."

"—what's his name?"

"Small. Small Gray. And I'm Ezola Gray. My other child is Dixie. Altogether we're the Grays of Richmond."

DIXIE GRAY.

The color that they wore.

You're not in Richmond twenty minutes you run smack into The Lost Cause. Ambulance pulls up, you get out, say thank you and shake hands, determine to your satisfaction ol' Orioles will pull through, look around and make a right instead of left and you're standing smack in front of the Museum of the Confederacy in what was once Jeff Davis's old White House.

It's like here's the hospital: here's the Confederacy.

Here's the present: here's the past.

Here's your x-rays: here's the funeral.

You can sense it here—The Past. Smell it from the river, in the cold smokestacks, through the abandoned sweet-scented brick tobacco drying houses. The Past is here, was here and never went. Outstayed itself.

Here's the march of science: here's the science of the march.

It's your pork, Virginia.

Soldiering, that is.

From a distance Richmond's skyline had cut a graphic glass and concrete profile on the dark horizon, names of banks blazing from their heights like pilot lights, the tallest buildings pointing to the district where the city makes and keeps its fortune. Twice, now, in a single day he'd approached a landmark capital by car, the two most important capitals of the former disunited states. Back then, Virginia's fortune was a black market— tobacco, cotton, slaves. Now it is the industry that calls itself Defense. Plants and bases—it seems the Army never left the Old Dominion, those ole soljurs just kept marchin out from West Point in the middle of the nineteenth century down into the war against the Mexicans, the Civil War, the War against the Indians.

45

what you worship, you become

All these Washingtons and Lees. Only now it's done from
Newport News on warships. Into Desert Storms. Your pork,
Virginia. Soldiering. It's what you worship. And what you wor-
ship, you become.

Holden had thought D.C. held the record for monuments per
capita but that was before he'd clapped eyes on Richmond. Have
to be as many dead soldiers on horses in this town as ever crossed
the wide Missouri heading for the wild wild West. Every street,
another soldier. GENERAL PIERRE GUSTAVE TOUTANT BEAUREGARD'S
name longer than his horse. In the six blocks he'd just walked from
the Museum of the Confederacy on Clay, down Tenth to the Old
City Hall on Broad, he'd counted thirteen statues. Now here he
was face to face (well, face to feet) with a bronze chorus line of
them, all Virginians, fanning out around the Greek-revival-style
state capitol. Patrick Henry. Thomas Jefferson. George Mason.
John Marshall. Walk through this square on a sweltering August
night like this, thinking about what your future might hold, and
these past giants jump at you. Stonewall Jackson for christ sake,
that Southern hero. Shot by accident by one of his own men. Ever
wonder why your side lost the war, Stonewall? No mystery there.
And in the center of all this? Our Father. Big George.

Holden sits down on a bench and stares at him.

George, geez, just sitting there astride this horse with your
seminal vesicles bronzed. Your uncontested little bronzed
booties. This one monumental bronze is supposed to be the most
priceless piece of statuary in the whole United States. How could
anybody know a thing like that for certain? Why put any mone-
tary value on it in the first place? In case it's stolen? Who would
steal it? Cuba? Samoa? For a ransom? And what's George doing
anyway? Why is he here? Why are any of them here? What is
Patrick Henry supposed to be reminding him? What's this statue

46

of George Washington trying to tell him? Think of me when you put on a wig?

Think of my wooden teeth and remember to floss?

Think of me before catching pneumonia?

Think of me when you lose to the North.

Think of me when you cross your next river.

Think of the memory of me outlasting my lifetime while you're going to die unmissed unremembered and unloved you stupid schmuck.

Almost heaven.

Somewhere there's a monument to the love that you haven't found yet, the love of your life and the shape of your future, discharging ions into our skin through the dark. She is the span of the rainbow you see before waking the first touch of air on your body each morning the word that you say without speaking the prayer that you made before life. She is the space of tomorrow

> the spill of conscience
> the fill of desire
> the spell of your name.

She is the love you remembered at birth the love you will make after dying. Somewhere it waits for you, love that is not of this earth. Where the sky ends. Where memory pales. Where eternity is. Almost heaven.

THE PLACE IS fucking *huge*.

There's a Nursing Education Building, Ambulatory Care Facility, Biochemistry Research Park, a gymnasium, a dental building, Magnetic Resonance Imaging Center, cancer center, heliport, Medical Library. Main Hospital. West Hospital. North Hospital.

Glass doors, your usual ground-floor information desk, tile floors with your ordinary white walls. Bank of elevators with your usual medical types in their green cotton medical robes. *Jesus* places like this make him jumpy. Hates them. Hospitals. Make him feel *sick*. And why do they always smell like beef gravy?

This is less intimidating than expected for a psycho ward. Pair of wooden doors, glass windows in their upper thirds, sign that says STAFF ONLY.

And the doors aren't locked, which seems a little strange. They open on a corridor that goes off to the left and right. And straight ahead there is a nurses' station like a soda fountain counter with a single nurse behind it like a waitress.

And in front of it, her back to him, a tall slim woman in a pair of faded jeans and a very baggy bright green sweater. In bare feet.

"—no, sorry, Johnnie," the nurse is saying to this woman, "he still hasn't called."

Nurse transfers her look to Holden as he approaches.

"—help you?" she inquires.

When the barefoot woman swings around.

With that way that beauty never fails to wallop its beholder. It hits him like lightning. What strikes him more than just her beauty—powerful enough, itself—is that rare but unforgettable phenomenon of immediately knowing more about a stranger than you can reasonably know, sensing intimate foreknowledge, its sudden new suggestion warming all your senses with the comfortable assurance of something that you've always known or were designed to know: hello, remember me? I'm the woman you've been waiting for. I'm the dream that you've been dreaming might come true.

On the three or four occasions this has happened to him in his life before, Holden's managed to form words, at least, and make coherent speech, managed to pretend it wasn't happening while all the symptoms of arousal went on pumping through his system, but this time this woman exudes something that shoots immediately, alarmingly, like a narcotic, through his skin into his bloodstream. He'd never dream of doing what he finds he's doing next, falling spell to what her eyes are asking, what her body wills his own to do: he stands so close to her their bodies touch. Her hands slide into his like water. Her eyes, turquoise and as startling as the turquoise eyes on peacock feathers, seem to hold the answers to all questions he could dare to ask while at the same time posing the only question he can't dare to answer. She parts her lips to speak, hesitates and blushes as two dark thinking lines, like punctuation marks, furrow on her brow. She casts her glance down, almost shyly, to where their fingers have entwined and starts to trace a pattern, as if writing him a message, across the taut skin of his hand. *Do you know me?* she finally whispers. His heart races. Not "Have we met?" or "Do I know you?" but "Do *you* know *me?*"—like that ad, what was it, that used to recycle those puffy-faced bloated has-been movie stars hawking an enhanced esteem and a believable identity via some plastic credit card. "*Do* you?" she repeats, those turquoise eyes pleading for an answer. And the truth is, standing there *this far* from pulling her against him and pressing his mouth onto hers, he feels as though he *does* know her, as if he's always known her. So, "—yes," he thinks. He feels light-headed. He nods. "—I think I do," he whispers, and for one breathtaking moment he feels completely unaware of anything but him-and-her, unaware of their surroundings, utterly unselfconscious, until, from somewhere along the periphery he sees someone approach and she, reacting, puts her hands up to his shoulders, leans her mouth up to his ear. He feels a spark against his cheek, feels the warmth escaping from her breasts against his chest. "—then tell them who I am," she breathes, tightening her grip around his shoulders as someone tries to lead her off. "Tell them who I am," she begs more loudly, as she's guided to step back from him.

Why is he surprised to have to suddenly realize she's a patient here? Seeing her standing here at first, her back to him, he thought she was a student—young and lithe, honey-haired and fresh-faced—but now he's forced to see her as she really is, see the lines around her turquoise eyes, those few strands of grey. Lithe, yes—and if not "fresh" of face, then full of health; but much older than he'd reckoned. Suddenly he sees she's not at all a woman near his age, but a woman closer to his mother's.

Holden blinks.

"—tell them who I am," she's saying, while a big guy in those green cottons medical orderlies routinely wear is gently leading her away.

Holden can't believe his eyes.

"—Melanie?" he utters.

"—*tell them!*" she pleads.

Doors open and close around her.

She disappears.

That's what I'm supposed to do, he is reminded. That's what I do. I tell people news. I tell them.

"—sir?" the desk nurse interrupts.

Holden turns her way.

"Sorry about that," she offers.

"—no problem," he says.

He pulls himself together.

"—this *is* the psycho ward," he rationalizes.

"*Is* it?"

She lets that rattle him before she says, "How can I help?"

"Dr. Graham," Holden tells her. "I'm his ten o'clock." He leans across the counter to survey the appointment book with her. "—yeah, here I am," he says, "but I'm not . . . ah . . . I'm not a patient."

She points him down the corridor and condescends, "Of course you isn't, hon."

The office door is open and before he can even start to enter, its entire frame is filled by a large, extremely tall man, simmering with vitality and brains—not at all the vision of the neurasthenic shrink Holden had expected. This one's young, prematurely bald, bearded, and kitted out in stylish linen pleated pants and a denim shirt to match his eyes, with sleeves rolled up.

Comic, Holden has the chance to think before the man's big handshake overcomes him. Because for the umpteenth time since he's been back in America he's aware of the crust of European stiffness and formality he's developed while he's been away. For this occasion, for example, what he'd done was haul out his one and only long-sleeved white shirt—and then he'd gone down to the gift shop in the Omni Hotel where he was staying first thing this morning and bought this stupid tie.

It's the kind of tie people who secretly despise you hope to see you buried in.

It has geese in green and tan in full flight with their necks elongated crapping all over it.

"—come in, come in," Dr. Graham's oozing, "—I am just *so* glad to meet someone who can finally connect me to the brother, I can't tell you—sit down, sit down—"

Holden does a quick take of the surroundings—an easy environment of controlled chaos, wall of books, television and video, a wall of windows overlooking the hospital entrance, and lots of pictures of three kids who are clearly the doctor's from the looks of them. Holden clocks no picture of their mom.

"—well I hope I haven't misled you about how much help I *can* be, Dr. Graham," Holden says, sitting down across from him at the ample paper-littered desk.

"—Alex, Alex, call me Alex," the doctor insists, "and you're not by any chance the son of that Holden Garfield I see writing in our *Newsweek*, are you?"

"—no sir," Holden says. "I *am* that Holden Garfield writing in your *Newsweek.*"

"—*no!* My daughter Georgia just did a Current Events report she stole from you! Wait till I tell her, she'll be thrilled!"

Hands Holden a framed snapshot from his desk of one of the same tall kids Holden's noted in the other photographs.

"She's my oldest." Alex smiles. "Well what the hell are you doing back on native shores, son? Why aren't you out there telling us what we need to know about our world?"

Even before the question's out he realizes he's struck a nerve and stops himself. Professionally, no doubt, Holden thinks, and shifts uncomfortably in his chair.

"—um, you'll forgive me, Dr.—"

"—Alex."

"Alex. I'm not here to talk about myself."

"You can let your guard down, son. Sometimes I actually ask questions out of personal interest."

Holden smiles, relaxes a little. Undoes the fucking tie. Takes from his pocket the other thing he'd bought in the gift shop that morning—a new notepad—and flips it open.

"I just ran into her out there," he says.

"Melanie?"

"I think so—I think it was her. Tall, thin, long hair—"

"—'beautiful'?"

Holden stares at him.

"Had you met her before?"

Holden shakes his head.

"Why did you think it was her?"

"I've seen her photograph."

"And what happened when you saw her?"

"What do you mean?"

"How did she react to you?"

"As if she knew me," Holden says.

Alex nods, as if he was expecting this.

"—*does* she?"

"Like I said, we've never—"

"I mean is there any way at all that she could be familiar with you through the brother—seen your picture, anything like that?"

"I doubt it—I mean it's possible but it's unlikely. Anyway, I thought the problem is she can't remember—"

"That's right. That's partly right. What she has—or what I think she has—what she's afflicted by is a type of event-specific amnesia—an involuntary differentiating forgetfulness. A self-censoring one."

Holden starts to write this down, then stops, self-consciously.

"There's a backdrop of reality in place," Alex continues, "a seamless reality of second-by-second time where she doesn't question things like today's state-of-the-art appliances or the advancing numbers on the calendar pages—but she's only one foot in the moment, so to speak. The rest of her is stopped twenty years ago in 1975. I *think*," he says. He runs both his hands over his head as if to refresh his thoughts. "I've agonized over this one, believe me. Believe me," he repeats. "When I try to inhabit her reality, live within the dimensions of her conscious mind, the nearest paradigm I can construct is something like a time sand-wich—one layer of real time on the bottom, 1975, and one layer of real time on top, 1995, with nothing in between but little bits of gristle in an over-processed filler, like time Spam. I've had everybody I could get my hands on who knew her these last twenty years come in and sit in the chair you're sitting in and tell me everything they could about her—her family doctors, the o.b. who delivered all her kids, kids' teachers, people from their neighborhood, the men who were in business with her husband, everyone, in fact, except the brother, whom I've come to think of as the key—to try to help me construct a working model of her personality, her integrated one, a psychological profile of Melanie between some time in 1975 and the twenty-seventh of June this year." Alex swivels in his chair to a low filing cabinet next to him and takes out a thick folder full of newspaper photocopies, which he hands to Holden. "And the best I can come up with so far is that she was *the* original soccer mom, the soccer mom to beat all

others. But entirely. Lived for nothing else but her husband and
those kids . . ."

Holden opens the file and is shocked by what he finds.

"—jesus," he murmurs.

"—oh, it was big news," Alex tells him. "Death of four kids?
Major local headlines."

Holden's hands shake as he reads through the *Richmond
Times-Dispatch* articles about the accident.

"Here's what I've been able to ascertain so far," Alex begins.
"The woman you just saw out there was born Melanie John at the
John Randolph Hospital in Hopewell, Virginia, on the morning of
the fourteenth of April 1950. She has an older brother, Noah John,
only two children of the union between Frederick Justice John and
wife Mary. Shortly after Melanie's birth Mary comes down with
polio, dies September 1952. Perfectly healthy childhood, all the
normal stuff, chicken pox, measles, high school, University of
Virginia. Then the kicker: *Law.* Father dead by then, has to work
her own way through, but finally takes her bar exam, passes it with
flying colors. Starts to clerk for a firm right here in Richmond.
This is one serious-minded woman—rooms alone, no boyfriends.
Seems to have spent her college years being educated, can you
believe. When one day—I still don't know how—into her life
walks a young carpenter just starting out in business building cus-
tom homes over in Chesterfield County named Jason Page and
bingo. Love. They marry, move into a little house out in
Midlothian, Melanie still works. For some reason which I'm still
not sure of she has no luck conceiving and they come in here to
MCV for fertility testing and she goes on a six-month hormone
treatment and gets pregnant for the first time in '78. Spontaneous
abortion second term. Same thing the next year. Then in '80 she
gets pregnant again and their first son, Thaddeus, is born in '81.

After that, it's pretty much just kids. Harris two years later. They move to a big house Jason builds in a development in Chester on the James River. Walker's born three years after that. Then Man, their little boy who was born three years ago, after she was forty." He rubs his head again. "And the last thing she remembers out of all that is how she felt when she passed her bar exam and working at the law office two blocks away from here on Broad Street. *Consciously* remembers," he amends.

Holden is slow on the uptake.

"—so . . . she doesn't remember any of this," he says, referring to the file in front of him. "—doesn't remember her children and husband are dead?"

Alex stares at him.

"Doesn't remember they ever existed."

Holden looks down at the pictures of the boys on the front page of the paper.

It takes him a moment to form the next question.

"—*permanently?*"

Alex leans back in his chair.

"Clinically, I'd wager not—but there's no way of knowing. Case studies prove amnesia is no stable state—it's organic—it's temporal, even—it shifts with time, comes and goes—but, chiefly, it goes. It deteriorates. If you think of amnesia as the dark twin of memory, then you can begin to understand how it works from your own experience of how your personal memories work. Memories deteriorate over time, resulting in forgetfulness, sometimes leaving fingerprints and sometimes not. Sometimes a memory can vanish altogether, other times it leaves its trace, it leaves you with a sense of loss, that you are missing something. Amnesia, on the other hand, when it deteriorates, deteriorates in the direction of *remembering*—that's why so many cases soon resolve to a state of full recovery of the lost memories. But how or when or even if that pattern of deterioration will evolve in Melanie, I have no way of predicting."

"Why don't you just tell her?" Holden asks.

Alex leans forward on the desk again.

"Right," he says. "How do you suggest I do that? Suppose I were to tell you—you, not her, *you*, in the healthy state of mind you're in—suppose I were to say to you, 'Holden, there's something you should know. Twenty years of your life have gone by that you can't remember. In the course of those twenty years you met and married the woman who was the great love of your life, had four children and lived in a domestic bliss beyond imagining. Then one day your wife and children were killed in a violent incident from which you managed to escape unharmed.' What would you do? Would you believe me? Why should you? Why would you even trust me after I told you something so horrific and farfetched as that? But what if I showed you these?" He points to the boys' pictures in the file. "What if I offered to show you 'proof'? What kind of 'proof' would it take to make you believe something is true if you can't remember it? Home movies? A trip to the now-empty family home? You tell me. You advise me what kind of shock tactics I should use—because when it comes to a theory that memory can be 'stirred' or memory can be 'jogged' or memory can be 're-awakened' or 'prompted,' let me tell you, son, there are hundreds out there, even thousands—and there are methods aplenty at my disposal—hypnosis, electric shock, psychotropic drugs—and I'm willing to give any or all of them a shot, believe me. But my first obligation is to her. It's not to The Truth, it's to The Patient. It's to that woman out there—and to tell you the God's Honest, before I can make an informed decision about what I can do to help restore her health, I have to have some idea *who she is*. Who the hell is she?

What kind of massive defense is at work that's brought on this amnesia? And why? I can give you her c.v. on paper—but what does that tell us? Her whole life—and I mean *her whole life*—her physical life, her mental life, her emotional one, her spiritual one—was that family. Period. They didn't belong to a church, they weren't really that close with their neighbors. They were warm out-going healthy people, an almost perfect family unit, but they were *self-contained*, they stayed to themselves. Whatever she was, *who*ever she was before she met Jason, that strong-willed independent girl who put herself through law school, got subsumed into the family unit. And I don't know what 'person' there is left. Who or what she feels and thinks she is. Historically, inside her sense of her life. Whether that 'person' is strong enough to face The Truth. That's why I need the brother. Need his help with this. Need to know about those early years, what shaped her. Need to know what only he can tell me, do you understand?"

Holden nods.

A silence falls between them.

The wail of a distant ambulance siren grows nearer.

"This is where you're supposed to start speaking," Alex prompts.

"—yeah, I know," Holden says, "I'm just thinking."

"—about?"

"About out there—at the nurses' station, when I first saw her. When I came in. I had the impression she was asking if there'd been any phone calls for her. Who would she be thinking they could possibly be from?"

"—the brother. From Noah. He's the only person that she talks to me about. She can't understand why she hasn't heard from him. It sounds to me like they're very close, but I can't tell whether that's the present speaking or the shadow past."

"Why don't you just tell her to call him?"

"I have. I encourage her to use the phone every time I see her."

"—and?"

"And she doesn't. She thinks he's on assignment somewhere and he'll call. She says he always does. Does he?"

"When I knew him, yeah. Like clockwork. Once a week. No matter where he was. Have you checked the house?"

Alex nods.

"But I admit when I went out there I wasn't looking for the brother. I was looking for clues about her, about who she is."

"Did you check the answering machine?"

"I didn't even notice if there was one. Maybe you can tell me why the brother's playing hard to find?"

"—um, yeah. It's a complicated story. But it's basically about a woman. The woman that he's with. Or might be with."

"What about her?"

"There are some people looking for her."

"Yeah, well, there are people looking for him, too . . ."

"Different kinda people. Do you have a key to Melanie's house?"

"No, there's a lawyer's office dealing with all that. I'll give you their card in case you—"

"—no, keep it," Holden says. "If I decide to get involved I'd rather stay away from lawyers . . ."

"—if you 'decide'? What are you undecided about?"

Holden fingers the file on the desk, takes a few moments to answer.

"I'm undecided about almost everything in my life right now, frankly. If you want to know. I kinda need some time to think things out—"

"—we don't have 'time,'" Alex emphasizes. He stands up. "Stay where you are—I want to show you something." He moves across the room, inserts a tape into the video machine and backs away from it toward his desk while he searches for the images he wants with the remote. "I hope this won't offend you," he tells Holden. On the screen a stop-frame grainy black-and-white image of a woman by herself in an empty room appears. As Alex starts the action he explains, "Some people are offended by surveillance-camera tapes as an invasion of privacy," and Holden sees the woman on the screen is Melanie. He stands up, too, next to Alex, so he can get a better look. "This is a couple of hours after the ambulance brought her in from where they were hit," Alex is saying. The image on the screen shows Melanie, barefoot, in a hospital shift, pacing back and forth, furiously moving her right hand in front of her. "We keep a couple rooms like this, with a surveillance camera, for patients under observation, in extreme distress . . ." He fast-forwards the tape a bit and says, "This is several hours later." The image shows her pacing, still, her hand cutting through the air like crazy. "This was basically her first response," Alex tells him, "—her *only* response. She didn't sleep, didn't eat. Didn't pee, didn't evacuate, didn't weep, didn't talk. Just paced back and forth, back and forth like this. Back and forth. Until on the third day I decided to sedate her."

"—what the hell's she doing with her hand?"

Alex slows the action down.

"She's writing," he tells Holden.

"—she's what? —wait, wait," Holden says. He stands closer to the screen and asks, "—can you slow it down some more?" so he can study it, then he gives a low long whistle. "Oh man," he murmurs, "you're not going to believe this, this is fucking weird.

61

But Noah *told* me his kid sister used to do this . . ." He turns around and sends a look toward Alex, then backs up to stand next to him again. "We were—where the fuck were we?—we were in Berlin, that was it. Noah and I were in Berlin—November 1989—the goddamn Wall had just come down and it was my first big story. We went together to Berlin but Noah let me have it. Let me write the story. Gave it to me. Anyway—I was really high. I was, like, flying—the whole place was on a high, it was electric, you could feel the emotion in the air like static. It was amazing. And I remember he and I stayed up all night two nights in a row and the second night we went out together and got really drunk, drunk as skunks, completely legless. Because—aside from everything else, the general euphoria—it was Noah's birthday. And somehow Melanie had figured out how to get a birthday message to him in Berlin and he was really thrilled to hear from her, really missing her I think because his relationship with that woman I told you about had gotten totally fucked up at that stage—anyway, it was Melanie and not the woman that he ended up talking to me about that night while we got drunk, about what a weird little kid she had been, how, after their mother died, she stopped talking. Instead of speaking, whenever she needed to communicate with anyone, instead of speaking she did this." He points to the screen. "—she *wrote*. Backwards, in the air."

"—it *is* backwards," Alex says. "—for her. But not to us. See?"

He starts the action up again and Holden watches as he traces Melanie's hand on the screen with his finger.

"—so what's she writing?" Holden whispers.

"What indeed . . . It was a mystery to me until I started tracing it—like this. I spent nights up here with sheets of plastic taped up on the TV screen transcribing it."

Holden watches him more closely.

"—this was all she'd do. Still wasn't sleeping, wouldn't eat, wouldn't talk, had no sense of self . . . no hygiene. So I administered sedation."

He shakes his head.

"—and when she woke up she had become *this* woman . . ."

He fast-forwards to an image of Melanie that Holden recognizes as the Melanie he'd encountered at the nurses' station.

"I'm not sure drugging her at that moment was the right thing for me to have done . . . I'm not even sure it didn't result in her present amnesiac state . . . but I had to take steps at that time to safeguard her physical health. I had to. But as a result of that induced sleep I created Sleeping Beauty in reverse. When she woke up all her princes were *dead* . . . Now look at this."

He fast-forwards again and they both step back a little for a better view.

"This was last week," Alex says.

"—*shit*," Holden breathes.

"—yeah, she's writing again. Only for brief moments and only once or twice a day but you can see what I mean about amnesia's decay and why I say there isn't time to delay? That defense mechanism that put her amnesia in place is already showing cracks like hairline fissures in the wall of a dam. I think The Truth is breaking through. Either that or this is the signature of a competing mechanism. A survival mechanism. Or a maternal one. Because what I was finally able to figure out is that these are her sons' voices breaking through, in what she's writing in the air. One by one I transcribed words—one by one I constructed sentences. Most of them were gibberish. Things like 'Nine's my lucky number.' Or—this is an actual transcription—'Okra makes me puke.' At first I thought the 'I' of these, the ego, was her own. But then it became obvious that there were multiple personalities at work and that what she was doing was writing out her children's histories. Getting them down in a mad unordered rush. Keeping those four boys in existence. Alive."

Holden watches the image of Melanie scribbling in air.

"Because if *she* doesn't keep the memory of her children alive," he starts to say.

"—no one will," Alex concurs.

Suddenly Melanie turns to the camera and looks directly into it, and Alex hits the pause button to freeze the image on screen.

"—so?" he asks Holden. "Will you find us the brother?"

Holden's distracted by the image on the screen and doesn't answer right away. Finally, embarrassed by the doctor's scrutiny, he murmurs, "I'll give it a try."

"—good!" Alex says.

He notes a self-conscious rush of color to Holden's complexion as he's caught in the act of staring at the face on the screen.

"—beautiful woman, isn't she?" Alex observes.

Holden nods.

He can't seem to take his eyes off the image of her.

"What else do you see there?" Alex says.

Holden blushes even more deeply.

"What do you mean?"

"In that face. In that look," Alex presses.

"I don't know," Holden fudges. "Something . . . I don't know how to say this, you've put me on the spot. Something sexy."

The air between them thins like the air at a high altitude.

"Does that make me nuts, or do you see it, too?" Holden asks the doctor. "Like there's a hunger there to go on living, a huge lust there for life."

"Or else," Alex concedes before he turns the system off, after they've both stared at her a minute, "this is what it looks like to be psychologically fearless. This is what you look like when there's nothing left for you to lose . . ."

DON'T HAVE TO BE A GENIUS to figure out their memorial is already constructed.

By the carpenter himself.

Standing empty now.

Not empty.

Locked.

Memories all locked inside.

Holden rents a car on Broad Street and drives back to the Omni to ditch the goose tie, change his clothes.

Because the heat's a curfew out there at high noon, everybody needed to be off the streets, and Holden needed some new clothes. The two pairs of jeans and three shirts in his knapsack are by now certifiably pathetic. And evoke a war zone. Evoke memories that way clothes do.

Like when you go home to your parents' house and open a drawer to find your mom has kept your team shirts from high school. And your one and only suit. And the ice skates you outgrew in seventh grade. Better do this, Holden's thinking and picks up the phone.

Sitting in his last pair of forlorn calvins on another hotel bed staring at his loafers in the corner. Which need new heels.

That familiar voice answers.

"—*hey, lovely,*" Holden says.

"—o my honey's voice!—how's my darlin boy?—where are you darlin?"

"I'm in the Colonies."

"—in the . . . one of the original thirteen?"

65

"—yup."

"—good heavens. —*why?*"

"—a story."

"—*where?*"

"Richmond."

"—Virginia? Only story in Richmond, Virginia, is whether or not they're goin to erect a bronze statue of Arthur Ashe as the first black man on Monument Avenue, that famous Great White Way. I mean why doesn't someone down there have the brassed balls to stand up and say at least his would be the first statue in that bronze pantheon that got the skin color approximately right—?"

Holden smiles.

"—so how ya doin, Kanga?"

"Don't change the subject. You're not really in *Richmond,* are you? Holden? Where are you, really? What's going on? Are they debriefing you at Langley?"

"—*mom.*"

"—what."

"I'm at the Richmond Omni. And Kanga? I'm registered *under my own name.*"

"You haven't been *shot* or anything have you? You're not locked up in a hospital ward somewhere—?"

"Earth to mom."

"—okay, *right.* Receiving."

"Let's talk about you."

"Okay. I'll drive down and see you."

Holden blinks.

"—okay?" she asks.

"—um . . ."

"—give myself a treat. Now that I have all this money from my divorce."

—oh *shit*, Holden thinks.

Now he had two things to do in his immediate future.

Find Noah.

And get a haircut.

IT FEELS LIKE I REMEMBER THIS, he realizes.

He's just come off the ramp in a full circle-and-a-quarter, four hundred and fifty degrees of spiraling concrete reinforced with steel: the exit off East Broad onto I-95. Every window in the car rolled down. Heading south. Toward Petersburg. Toward North Carolina. Toward Florida. A fucking Peterbilt in black and chrome, behemoth, thundering down behind him.

Ahead: a heat-inversion sky, pale and motionless as somebody in a faint.

Beneath it, highway gantries, white on green.

Then the sky again, so white it hurts his eyes.

Then the river, unmade bed exposed.

The bridge.

The old clock in the spire of the old train station.

Along eight gently curving canted lanes of road. All combining—the sky, the signs, the river, bridge, the old brick spire and the road—into this picture, a group portrait, our national profile, the American landscape, the American road, picture-framed in an American windshield.

That's why Holden feels like he remembers this—not because he's seen this view before, but because all views like this one are familiar, part of the communal memory of all of us who travel down these highways between cities in our cars. *Christ*, he thinks, it could be Houston, could be Hartford. Could be the road that comes up on the screen in computer games. Could be.

If he was only half-way paying attention to it. If he put himself on autopilot, let his conditioned reflexes and not his full attention do the driving. And suddenly he realizes that this feeling he mistakes for remembering is not remembering at all. It's recognition. Recognition, yes; but not remembering. There's a difference, after all, between knowing and remembering. Isn't there? A difference between knowing what a river *is* and remembering a specific river. Isn't there? Like, for instance, he now thinks, he can *remember* the Mississippi, the way it looks where it begins its turn into the delta from New Orleans—he can see it in his mind. He can see the Seine, the way it looks from the quai beside the Hotel de Ville, all lit up at night. He can see the Nile. He can see the Danube, fucked and filthy in Romania, reeking, even in his mind, of scum and blood and sewer. He can remember the Hudson, the Potomac and the Rio Grande (its name a joke), even the Chicago—all the rivers that he's seen. But he can only "recognize" the river he's now crossing. Only "know" that it's the James—not "remember" it. Only know it has to be the James because he knows, not from experience, but because he has been taught to know, that the river that's the port of Richmond is the James. And he remembers now—picking up his speed and tuning in to Radio Virginia Country 109.00 AM— he remembers every time they drove across a river on a highway his father *Pooh* that pompous bastard in the front seat would nod his head and tell his son and wife, "Every river is an economics lesson."

Until, one day near the end, Kanga turned to him and snapped, "Oh, shut up. The only thing you need to know about a river is that every river is *a way out.*"

AMNESIA is the loss of the ability to travel time.

Amnesia's *now*. And only Now. And maybe Later. Never *then*. The opposite of Never-Never Land where little boys and girls never have to do the business and grow up. Where being children, one and all, is all there is to do. Where being a forever child is every baby's future.

After fifteen miles on I-95 he exits at Route 10 toward Hopewell—*95 to 10*, he thinks, like someone going back in years from an advanced age to his childhood—and three miles down Route 10, over on the left, across the median, he sees the sign.

WELCOME TO RIVERS END A PLANNED COMMUNITY.

Welcome to suburbia.

He had torn the whole page from the phone book, a sloppy habit in a free country such as this, but one he didn't want to break, even now, even back here in the States, because he'd picked the habit up from Noah way back when, when he was very green, and it reminded him of how he was back then.

Never carry any notes you've written in your pockets.

Never write addresses down.

If you have to write one down in order to remember it, hide it among other things that camouflage it.

A phone number written like you're adding something in a segmented two-digit column.

That way when they stop and search you, when they go through all your things, at least your nerves will know you tried your best to hide your sources.

He'd ripped the whole page out in his hotel room because if he was going to track Noah, he didn't want to call the lawyers. He didn't want to leave a trail. No time, then, to think about how

69

dumb it was. The address, that is. But now, sitting in the front seat of the rented car pulled up on the side of the entrance road, he looks at it, then he looks out the window. Then he looks at it again. One, three, four, followed by two zeroes Wanda Circle. 13400 *Wanda* Circle? Thirteen *thousand* and four hundred "Wanda"?

Slowly, very slowly, he begins to cruise the neighborhood.

Looking for a street called Wanda.

Well, a circle, really.

Knowing all the while that once he finds it he's almost certainly going to have to figure out the best way to break in. Case it out. Come back after dark. If they catch him he can always say he's on a secret mission from the psycho guy at MCV. Or that his father—you won't find him in the phone book, officer, his name is Pooh—works for the government and hangs like *this* with Clinton.

But he can't find it.

Rivers End Road, the entry road, runs to Rivers End Court on the left and Rivers End Circle on the right, then T-junctions at Rivers End Terrace. To the left, Scrimshaw Drive, Furlong Circle, Redwing Terrace. To the right, more of the same, every street named for a dream pursuit, a hobby or a bird; every two-acre lot lorded over by a brand-new manor, every brand-new manor carefully constructed in the manner of an older one—a new "Colonial," new "Greek Revival," new Plantation, new Spanish Mission. Why do Americans go to so much effort to make new houses look like fake antiques? he wonders. Isn't this a little scary? What does it say about a place that tries so hard to look like something from the past? Why would someone want to try to paint a house in the last decade before the year 2000 so it looks the way they think it might have looked in a tobacco field infested with mosquitoes in the eighteenth century when paint was made with lime and clay and ash and piss instead of vinyl? Only in America could the word *antique* become a verb, he thinks. A transitive one. Let's not wait for time and tides to do it, hon— let's antique. Let's antique *it*. Let's give it *its antique look* right away. And stick a couple wooden ducks out on the lawn.

He'd forgotten just how dire all this is.

How curious a car-dependent ethos is.

All this, he thinks—and no real place to go, because in this community everything is private. There is no "public." August afternoon, the height of summer—where are all the kids? Where, in fact, is anybody? All the time that he's been going round in circles, he hasn't seen a single person—not even another driver in another car. No signs of life—just street signs. SPEED LIMIT 25. BUILT TO SUIT. He hadn't expected it to be like this. Where she lived. Although now he can begin to understand how you could live here, live a stone's throw from your neighbor, and still feel isolated. The road he's on ends abruptly in a mound of sand on a field of scrappy weeds and cornflowers. In front of the sand pile there is a signpost with an ornate sign attached to it, scrolled top and bottom to look like the Declaration of Independence. It has two arrows painted on it, one pointing back in the direction from which he's come, toward the words SALES OFFICE. The other arrow points straight up, off the sign, Holden notes, smiling for the first time in an hour, toward Heaven, over the words FUTURE NEIGHBORHOOD.

THE SALES OFFICE is a white clapboard farmhouse affair with black shutters and a porch. Next to the door is a bin with brochures in it and the instruction *Take One*, so he does. A RIVER

something happened here

RUNS BY IT he reads on the front. "Golf. Tennis. Swimming. Boating. Whatever your pleasure, you'll get more out of life in Rivers End." On the inside there's a map.

Wanda Circle, he discovers, is about a half mile away, on the far side of the golf course, among a latticework of streets called Kimberly, Janine and Tracy, as if the planners of this perfect place had exhausted their ornithological taxonomy and just said Fuckit, momma, let's call the rest of these here streets after the kids. Its four two-story residences stare across the Circle at each other over miraculously green front lawns, except for one, the second on the left, which commands a view from its rear prospect of the confluence of the Appomattox and the James, but faces the Circle amid what has become a parched brown field of knee-high weeds and wild seed-bearing grass. Even if you didn't know the story, Holden thinks, you would know that something happened here, to the people in this house, that hadn't happened to the others. He pulls into the driveway and gets out. Above the river something ominous is rising, the usual August afternoon thundercloud. There's not a trace of a breeze. Insects buzz. The air is still, and very close.

"Can I help you there?" a woman's voice calls behind him. She's standing with her arms crossed over her chest in the open doorway of the house next door.

"—oh —hi," Holden says. "—don't mind me, I'm just—"

"I do mind you," she says. "That's private property you're on."

"—yes I know, I—"

"—and you're makin me let a lot of this hot air into my kitchen just to find out what you're doin."

"—oh. I'm sorry," he says and starts to move across her yard toward her. In a flash she's outside her kitchen door onto the deck, the kitchen door slammed shut behind her, pointing a small canister at Holden.

"—whoa," he says. He stops and puts his hands up. "—what are you gonna do there, lady, set me on fire with your lighter?"

"It's Mace," she says.

"—Mace! What are you doing with Mace? Wait—*wait, wait, wait—*"

She's started toward him, backing him toward his car.

"—hold on a second, I'm a friend of Melanie's . . . well not Melanie's exactly, her brother . . . I used to work with him—"

He bumps into his car, recoils from the hot surface. "—ow!"

The woman stops. "What's her brother's name then?"

"Noah John for christsake."

"Where did you work with him?"

"In London. Geez, I think I gave myself a first-degree burn here."

"Turn around," she says. "Nope, it's nothin." She runs her hand across his ass. "Didn't even brown the fabric. But if you want to go inside and check you can use the powder room . . ."

"—so are we being friendly now?"

She nods.

They exchange their introductions.

"I'm afraid I have some bad news for you Mr. Garfield," she explains, "about Melanie an' all."

"I know," Holden tells her. "I've just come from MCV."

"Oh we've been there. I took her in some clothes. We were asked a lot of questions by that doctor. Wouldn't let us see her though."

"Why not?"

"Paul—that's my husband—Paul says the reason was I was just too jumpy, but I couldn't help it. Not a day goes by I still don't break down at least once when I think about it."

"I take it you were close," Holden observes.

"—well, we were neighbors. Their kids played with ours."

Holden feels the sweat run down his legs.

"You must have a key, then," he suggests.

He expects more resistance from her than she shows. In fact, she doesn't even ask him why or what he's looking for. Instead, she retreats into her kitchen, returns with the key and leads him through the house stepping to one side, against the wall, when they enter each room as if she's showing him around—a prospective tenant—and he quickly realizes she's not really aware of him, that she's communing by herself with something he can't see, that she's pressed herself into the corners of this house not to spy on him or to watch him but to give the memories this house contains their ample space.

As if that's possible, Holden thinks.

Because he feels the force of them immediately.

Hard to explain, the presence of memory, because, like gravity and time, it's invisible, its existence leaving only secondary proofs, the way a boulder barreling down a mountain is proof not only of its own material thing-ness but—more weightily—of *gravity's*.

His mother, more than anyone he's ever known, is especially attuned to these invisibles. Several times when he was growing up he would come home from school and find her grieving, absolutely hopeless, beside herself with nonspecific sadness, and then three hours later they'd turn on the Evening News and hear about the earthquake in Armenia killing hundreds that day.

It was Kanga, too, who gave him the only foolproof antidote to fear he knew. Worked for him each time in every situation. Because she had once come into his bedroom at night and found him crying. When she asked him what the matter was and he told her he was scared because he could feel the presence of something

74

in his room with him in the dark, she said, "—oh is that all? Go back to sleep. Everybody feels that way when they brush too close to God."

Then and every time thereafter—even under fire in a war zone—the instant he was gripped by fear he was also touched by the conviction that he'd brushed too close to his Protector and so was in the best of company for facing down his demons.

But what was waiting for him in the house on Wanda Circle was a force unlike others he'd encountered, even on that killing field of Srebrenica.

What was waiting in the house was life, not death.

Life-after-death; a family's life preserved, like an organ in a jar.

Just inside the back door: six pairs of boots.

Six ranks of pegs mounted on a wall six rows deep, a name identifying every row above the top peg. The usual array of baseball caps and jackets. Mess that boys collect. One weather-battered straw sun hat with a light blue satin ribbon, a bouquet of lavender and chamomile tucked in its band.

To the right—the laundry. Industrial, almost; two washers and two dryers. Two ironing boards. A sink. A jar of hand cream, bar of Lava soap. Clothes baskets on the terra-cotta floor. Detergents. Box marked FOUND IN POCKETS.

To the left inside the back door—Jason's office. Drafting table. Rolls of blueprints. Pens and pencils. Answering machine with a green light blinking. Framed flyer from a realtor— "Welcome to 13400 Wanda Circle!"—with a full description of the house. Pegboard. A spirit level on the top shelf. Its unblinking watery eye.

Then the whole shock of the kitchen.

Nothing, literally nothing, it would seem, had been touched or moved since the morning of their deaths, including dirty breakfast dishes in the sink and a pan of bacon drippings on the stove—a fusty smell, a combination of soured milk, decaying fruit and vegetables, bread mold and rancid butter in the sealed, hot room.

"It's like an oven in here," he says. To his consternation it comes out in a whisper. "Can't we open a window or something—let some air in?"

The neighbor shakes her head.

"We have to keep it locked up."

"Why?"

"It's what the lawyers said. For the insurance."

"—well let's turn a fan on or something, get some air circulating . . . start to clean some of this up . . ."

She puts a restraining hand on Holden's.

"It's not right," she whispers.

"—what are you talking about?"

"We should leave it as it is. The way she left it. The way that she'll remember it when she comes back."

She isn't coming back, Holden almost tells her, but the woman's eyes have gone a little weird, a narrow ring of brightness has appeared around her pupils.

"—the lawyers gave us some instructions," she volunteers.

Holden moves away from her, moving around the kitchen slowly, but she follows him, trailing her concerns.

"—they said, 'Don't touch anything—not a thing' until this mess can be worked out—you know, she inherited all this from Jason's will but, well," she says, "she's not in any shape to know what she's going to do with it just yet and meanwhile there's the cost of everything, the cost of maintenance, the hospital, the funeral costs—"

"—there were funerals?"

"One. The lawyers decided. A combined one. I mean, there were so many things to think about. What to do about the phone for instance. What to do with all the mail. So many things nobody ever thinks will happen. An' then of course no help from the brother. No word from him at all—"

"Why are there two answering machines?" Holden interrupts her.

"—what?"

"—two answering machines. One in Jason's office, one in here. Why?"

She's looking at him like he's asked her something in a foreign language.

"Separate lines?" he asks. "That would make sense, one for the business, one for the house—"

"—three," she says. "The boys have one. For their computers."

Holden picks the handset up, but the line's been disconnected.

"—what about these messages?" he asks her. "Why's the light still blinking?"

"It's been like that . . . since . . ."

"—since when?"

"—from the beginning."

"—you never checked them?"

"—like I told you the lawyers gave us these instructions not to touch anything, so we haven't . . . except to pick their clothes out for the—what are you doing?"

Holden lifts the tape out of the answering machine. "Where are the computers?" he asks, but doesn't wait for her to answer. From the kitchen he follows the logic of the layout of the house

what he is after

to a central hallway and the stairs. *Think of this as just another job* he tells himself, stopping on the landing. Because he knows which bedroom he will come to first.

In the house that he grew up in, Pooh and Kanga occupied the back bedroom because they wanted privacy, they didn't want their son to have to pass their door last thing at night, first thing in the morning. But when you have four kids, he reckons, the strategic location would be between their bedrooms and the exits—and he isn't wrong, although the room, itself, is not what he expects. Against his will, it draws him in. Because it's simply beautiful. Its far side, a side wall of the house, is faced, floor to cathedral-height ceiling, in a creamy sandstone, into which a hearth is set, with two hand-carved rocking chairs on either side, magnificently turned and engraved, no doubt, by the groom himself with their names, the date of their wedding and the words *For Eternity.* Beiges—nothing frilly on the bed. Grey slate floor instead of carpeting. More like a mountain lodge than a suburban bedroom, a place to swap tales at the end of a long day in the saddle.

Except it holds a trace of lavender.

Outside, there's a skittering across the roof and beyond it he can sense a larger commotion gathering above the house.

"I was afraid of this," the woman warns, coming up the stairs. "I gotta run get Buddy from the Little League, it's gonna storm."

"—just let me check one more thing," Holden tells her.

The first bedroom seems to be the youngest boy's—Man's—and the second and the third have only a PlayStation and a Nintendo installed. But in the farthest bedroom Holden finds what he is after.

"I'm sorry but you'll have to go now, Mr. Garfield," the neighbor is saying.

78

"—give me a sec, all right?"

He turns the computer on and waits to see what it delivers.
Windows.

"—thank you, Mr. Gates," he sighs. "You beauty . . . 'Mail
Center,' come on, you can do this . . . oh, hello gorgeous . . . *yes!*"

With a terrifying noise like a crevasse opening the room is
bathed in the silver glow of summer sheet lightning; and the
power momentarily snaps and fails.

"—*please,*" she urges.

"—right, right, damn, shit, sorry, sorry—*thank you,*" he says.
He takes her hand. "—you don't know how much help this has
been . . ."

Outside everything is touched by eerie pale green light.

"—this is hailin weather," the neighbor says to Holden,
"—always gets like this before a hail. Poor Buddy, he must think
I've forgotten him . . ."

Holden goes as far as her driveway with her and watches her
get in her car.

"—are you going to be all right, Mrs. Wallace?"

She has a haunted look.

"Since all this?" she says nodding toward the house next door.
"You understand I can't but help be scared for all my children."

Holden leans against her car, strangely touched by her sense
of helplessness.

"I need to come again tomorrow," he tells her.

"—oh I wish you didn't."

"Don't you like me, Mrs. Wallace?"

"—no, I just mean . . ."

She starts the ignition and the wipers automatically go on.

"—well can you make it in the mornin? I have to run Leeann
to the dentist at eleven."

ice

"—how 'bout I come at ten?" Holden asks, just as stuff begins to bounce off the car and in the driveway, all around them, on the yard.

They look at it, speechless with amazement.

Holden holds a hand out and one lands in his palm.

"—well did you ever?" Mrs. Wallace breathes. "This musta gone straight up outta somebody's garden—"

Holden stays there when she leaves.

Staring at the sky.

Because it's thundering.

And dropping frozen peas from heaven.

A HAILSTORM strikes the way a plague of locusts does in the Bible; like a tornado does—in a band. You can be standing over there on the eighth hole halfway around the course, about to swing onto the ninth, and a light rain might start to fall where you are while over at the next hole a shaft of graupel will be rattling, rat-a-tatting turf with icy grapeshot. Hail falls from a single cumulonimbus thundercloud, called a cell, and the ground area swept by its shaft is known as the hailstreak, typically about a hundred feet wide, unless building into super-streaks called hailswaths. The largest hailswath recorded so far swept across 788 square miles of Illinois in 1968 unloading 82 million cubic feet of ice on that patch of the Land of Lincoln in ninety minutes. In July. And Padge, Holden's crazy old grandfather, used to fill Holden's impressionable mind with stories like "Hail—the Conquering Hero," about how hail had saved the Fourth of July out in Cheyenne, "The Capital of Hail," one sweltering summer in the 1880s in a drought when the town didn't have enough water to make ice for ice cream for the celebration, till it hailed.

And it was Padge who, before Holden had ever even thought about traveling all around the world or becoming a journalist, taught him his first necessary lesson about disaster's size, how to gauge a disaster in human terms, not numerical ones, by telling him the series of tales called "Death by Hail" about how DEATH BY HAIL headlines from China or India were always huge—where hundreds of people in Hunan Province or the Punjab died when hailstones the size of grapefruits fell like citrus bombs on rice paddies and tea terraces conking hundreds on their noggins where they toiled in their pajamas, killing scores of innocents en masse not because the storm was more severe—stupid headline writing idiots!—not because the hailswath was wider or the streak more lethal but because there are more bodies on the ground in those places to begin with, because of human density: you can run that same storm back and forth across someplace like Montana or Saskatchewan a whole year and maybe, because the laws of statistics weight it that way, maybe, Padge told him, you will kill, just maybe, a trout. That's why it was so memorable one morning when Padge showed up at the house clutching a *Boston Globe.* His fly was open, as usual in his final years, and he hadn't shaved and his cheeks looked like those cacti with big white needles stuck in them like pin cushions. DEATH BY HAIL, the headline said. "Where's the boy?" Padge demanded, faced with Kanga at the door.

"—for godsake, Padge, pull the zipper up, you look like a—"
"—*see this?*" he posed, poking the paper at Holden.
"—'Death by Hail,'" Holden read. "'Fort Collins, Colo—'"
"—rado. *Colorado.*"
"'A three-month-old infant was killed yesterday in Fort Collins—Colo*rado*—as it slept in its mother's arms when hailstones fell on it during a picnic, police sources report—'"

"—*see?* —*that's* worth reporting! Say what you will about That sonofabitch The Almighty, but The Bastard can *aim* when He wants to!"

Although most of the time He doesn't, Holden had learned.

Most of the time things occur in the absence of aim: without meaning.

Or maybe not most of the time.

Maybe always.

At the bend in the road where Wanda Circle opens out onto Dionne Drive along the golf course beside the river, he can see the path of the hailstreak where it dropped a sheet of white over the golf course as if another Ice Age had encroached upon the sandtraps down the fairway, across the road, and disappeared into the pine woods on the right. In its path, in the middle of the road, it had stranded a golf cart, which Holden brakes abruptly to avoid running into broadside. Beneath his tires hail-stones pop.

They crunch when he walks over them.

"You okay?" he asks the couple in the golf cart. They're, like, in their seventies, he thinks. They're holding hands and the woman's pressing a Kleenex to her forehead where she's bleeding through a single tiny spot like an erupted blemish.

"Oh hello dear," she says to Holden. "We're just waiting for the poor thing to regain its senses."

She points with the balled-up Kleenex toward the golf course.

Standing on the nearest green, splay-legged and so thin you could almost miss it in the landscape, is a shivering fawn.

The sight of a thing so out of context, so vulnerable against a manmade landscape, rivets Holden.

"Well," the old gent breathes, low sun breaking through trees behind them, "we're ideally placed to catch the rainbow, mother."

82

Across the James, its five tall thrusting yellow stanchions picking up the sun, is a magnificent bridge, the sight of which Holden had failed to notice on his way in.

"—golly what's that?"

"That's the new Varina-Enon bridge there on 295," the old guy tells him. "Evening it opened mother and I drove back and forth across it half a dozen times—"

"—that was lovely," she confirms.

"—nice view from there, you oughta drive it."

"—the 'Varina'—?"

"Enon."

"Enon," Holden repeats.

"Old Testament," the woman says. "This is the Enon district of the county. It's what our local school is called."

"—and 'Varina'?"

"—well, oh my dear! You're not from around these parts then are you?"

"—no ma'am."

"Varina's the beloved name of our departed President's widow."

Holden ruminates a mo.

Before the penny drops.

"—*no,*" he laughs.

"—well it's a place name, too," the old gent argues.

"—but the place was named for her," the woman prompts.

"And you don't think that's strange?" Holden asks them, and they stare at him. "—naming a bridge after his *wife?* I mean—not even after Jefferson Davis, himself, after the President of the Confederacy, but after his *wife?* That doesn't seem . . . strange? I mean—not even after Mamie or Eleanor, you know, the wife of a *real* President . . . Hillary—there you go. Or Nancy. Jackie O . . ."

They all three crack up at that one.

"—guess not," Holden admits.

North or South, it doesn't matter.

After Chappaquiddick you'd have to be insane to name a bridge after a Kennedy.

Inside every building, Holden has long known, is a ruin—its ruin, waiting to get out.

Maybe inside every person, too, he now considers.

If they live long enough.

Like that couple he'd just seen—how weird was that? Coming across a pair of old guys like that who'd been married since Day One right after leaving that house where all the rooms had been turned into still lifes, museum-ized on the spot by a stroke of cruel luck.

It gave him the willies, that house.

It made him feel like a trespasser, which it should.

Made him feel like a voyeur.

Like a reporter.

He'd tried not to let the kids take shape at all, tried not to imagine them, feel their presences, their personalities, tried to keep them faceless in his mind while he went through the place. And maybe it was the fucking orphaned fawn out on the golf course, the sight of it, so vulnerable, that had ripped through his pretense. Maybe not. Maybe it had been that other moment, not the moment he had seen the isolated fawn out on the golf course, but the moment that he caught the old couple holding hands, the way their skins looked on the backs of their hands—tight and smooth and falsely young. Maybe it was then it hit him that those boys were *gone*, it didn't matter what they looked like, didn't matter whether he could animate them in his mind or not, they were *gone* and they would never grow up or grow fond or grow old. They were dead—what did it matter that he'd never known them? What kind of half-dead person had he become that he tried to keep the dead at bay, erase them even further, bury them *plus* make them invisible? *Fuck this*, he thinks, what's happened to my life? When did I become *my job?* Where did *my life* disappear to? I'm not a person anymore I'm a fucking knee jerk waiting for a hammer, what a fucking laugh this is, I'm the knock-knock joke with no one home, no one fucking there to answer the big question.

And he begins to cry—even though his tears are way past due—not like he cried the other day in the hotel room, not fueled with alcohol and sexual self-pity—he begins to cry because he feels afraid and for the first time since he was little Kanga's brush with God doesn't work its magic, Kanga's little homily about brushing up too close to the Eternal One doesn't do the trick because, quite frankly, right now if Holden came that close to God, if there was One up there, Holden would haul off and punch Him in the nose.

He pulls off the road to pull himself together and finds himself in the driveway of a deserted motor lodge, a couple dozen cabins scattered through the woods, built, from the looks of them, back in the thirties when this highway was built, and called, according to the dilapidated weather-ruined sign, the "trick Henry." No doubt, Holden reflects, brightening a little, the same "trick Henry" of "Give me liberty or give me you-know-what" fame. Good ol' Pat, he thinks, another ol' embalmed Virginian who hadn't seen it coming, hadn't even known he never had the choice because, Holden tells himself as he steers slowly down a weedy track past some cabins into the pines, it was never give me liberty *or* give me death. "Where'd you get the fucking 'or' Pat?"

he asks out loud, coming to a stop. "It's give me liberty *and* give me death," he says, " 'cause death is in there from the start. On your dance card. Death is what you get for breathing." He turns the engine off but leaves the key turned in the ignition. Picks up the tape from the answering machine and holds it in his hand a second, considering how weird this is about to be. They are dead and he is going to listen to the messages they were supposed to hear. He plays through both sides until he's sure he's heard everything that's on there—listening especially for anything from Noah, whose voice he knows he'll recognize at once. In his heart he always knew Noah is too smart to leave so obvious a trail— since he disappeared, if Noah ever used the phone at all to be in touch with Melanie and the members of her family, Holden guesses Noah would have called only on pre-arranged days at pre-arranged times, so he's not surprised when he doesn't hear his voice—in fact, he's relieved. If he's going to get his lead to Noah from her house—and he knows in his reporter's bones that he's going to—it's going to come from the boys' computer because it's easier to hide your identity there, hide your name, your gender, everything about yourself except the way you choose to write. What he'll have to do tomorrow, when he goes back there, is run a jack line from the neighbor's telephone, from Mrs. Wallace's kitchen, across the yard to the boys' computer, and check through the new e-mail and the filed messages for Noah's written voice, which is as distinctive as his speaking voice and which Holden knows he could recognize at once.

In the meantime he does something he knows is not a healthy thing to do.

He rewinds the tape and listens to the last three messages again—old ones, left there at the tag end of a string of messages erased under more recent ones. Then, in what he knows is a form of desperate or compulsive behavior, he listens to them again. And again. Until, in the middle of the sixth or seventh replay, he forces himself out of the car, as much to escape from the seductive power of their voices as to prevent himself from giving in again. He walks from the car toward one of the deserted cabins and sits down on its rotted doorstep and watches a spider waiting in its web, until he hears the voices stop and the tape wind to its end and finish.

It takes a while for the silence that falls on the place to replace the sound of the boys' voices in his mind. What is it about a voice that reveals so much of the identity of its speaker? It's not its sound, alone, especially in voices young as these. All kids' voices sound the same, he thinks, don't they? Except maybe to their parents. To their mothers. Still, all you need is one kid in a crowd to call out "Mom!" then just watch how every mother turns around. All three of these boys' voices had been different in their own way, he supposes, but he'd be hard-pressed to identify any one of them with certainty out of a group of, say, ten. Except the boy's voice that was going down, growing deep, fathoming the first depths of his manhood. He guesses that one must be—what's his name?— the oldest. Her oldest son. Families work that way, he realized: they don't need to identify themselves to each other, they don't need to say, "Hi, this is your oldest son," they just speak. They just say, "Can you come and get me?" or "I forgot that form I need upstairs on my desk" or "Are you there, Mom? *Yo*—Mom? Okay—you're outside or something—Dad says to tell you we got the thing but it took forever and we're running late. So I hope you get this before you start to freak. Okay—yeah, if Matt calls tell him he should go to Jamie's and I'll catch them there when I get home. Or vice versa. I mean, if Jamie calls before. You know what I mean—Dad's waving, bye! See ya!"

loneliness

All that random debris—a universe of it—all that ferocious mess, that focused intensity, that goes into family life: Holden had missed out on that as an only child. He agonized about it— he still does, sometimes—what it must be like to have that built-in noise, that built-in rough-and-tumble, built-in remedy for loneliness. Looking around at this place, now, for the first time in the fullness of its silence, he reckons maybe that's why places like this, the early road stops, used to be built this way, like camp-sites, before privacy and fear became our social contract, before alienation became the air we breathe, instead of campfire smoke. Places like this one, he starts to see, standing up and taking it all in, *were* a kind of artificial family, a place to lay over, modeled on a family house where each unit was a kind of separate bedroom where you could keep your door open if you wanted to or wander out where there was cooking going on and sit down in the middle of it until somebody talked to you, just like at home in the family kitchen. As he walks around between these cabins, looking into them through the broken windowpanes, he realizes he's seen this place before, or some place like it, in movies from the thirties and the forties—a place like this, built to offer false security, fake hominess, a place with built-in neighbors, full moon playing through the trees, a mix of Tommy Dorsey and cicadas, smell of shallow sump pump and a brace of eggs fried up with onions . . .

In the center of the group of cabins there are still some pic-nic tables around a stand of birch trees, and all around the bark of them, as if written on scrolls, there are dates carved into the trees. And names. Initials. Why this should make him sad all of a sudden Holden doesn't know at first, until, as he traces a name in the bark with his finger, he remembers that other bark back in Bosnia that baby had been nailed to. He remembers the woman

88

who had come up to him in a village a couple days later, too, just appeared out of nowhere with these torn pictures she kept forcing on him. "She says these are her sons," the translator told him. "She says they're missing. She says they have been missing from this village for over a year."

"What does she want me to do?" Holden asked him, impatiently. "I can't do anything. Tell her to keep them," he told the translator. "Tell her to keep them for herself."

Holden remembers the way that the woman wouldn't be shrugged off, how she just wouldn't give up, how some simple indomitable force kept her by his side, tugging on him, stumbling to keep up, forcing her pictures on him.

"Tell her I can't help," he finally said, stopping again, this time in anger. "What am I, *Wendy*? I'm not in the business of finding *lost boys*—"

"—just *take them*," his translator pleaded. "They are dead. She knows that they're dead. She doesn't need these photographs to remind her of them. She doesn't need their kind of reminding. She just needs to know where her sons have been buried. She just wants to know where to go with her candles."

Into the dark, Holden now thinks. He leans down and picks up a rock, a sharp piece of quartz that will cut like an arrowhead. Into the dark, he repeats to himself, beginning to carve Melanie's sons' initials. Into the blackness, you stupid woman, he thinks, carving them deep, all four of them, so they'll last. Where the hell else are we supposed to take candles?

ONE THING ABOUT CHESS, see, is it's all black and white.
. Unlike life.

Thing about chess is nothing happens by accident.

Move here and you're Kasparov.

Move over there and you're fucked.

You can't *run into* a move by mistake.

A move doesn't *fall* on you—there it is, the whole thing laid out in front of you, no secrets kept. You lose, it's your fault, plain and simple. No coincidence, no sudden corners you can't see around. No one to blame but yourself.

So maybe his next move should have been a drink before dinner.

On his lonesome. All by himself.

But instead, after dropping the car off at the Omni he finds himself strolling back up the hill past the state capitol, hospital-ward, on the pretense that maybe he'd catch Dr. Graham—Alex—for a beer before the good doctor went home.

"Uh-*huh*," the same desk nurse from this morning reassesses. "So are we still not a patient or are we here to commit ourself this time?"

Holden turns on his understated charm. "Any chance the doctor is in?"

"No, hon, he's long gone." She points a finger in a direction that he hasn't been yet and says, "—but Johnnie's been looking for you."

"'Johnnie' has," Holden repeats. "Who's Johnnie?"

She looks at him as if You devil, you.

"Your girlfriend," she prompts.

When Holden still doesn't get it she adds, "From this morning?"

"—oh." Holden wakes up. Melanie *John*. "Johnnie." A nick-name.

"I got a clearance here for you from Dr. Graham so you can go on and have a short visit if that's what you want. She usually sits out on the terrace this time of evening. Down there, through the TV room. I just have to get you to sign here . . ." He does. "And remind you we close shop at eight."

Had he intended this?

Your move, he tells himself.

She's standing there, he can see her through the glass doors in the TV room, alone out on the terrace in front of a big wooden table with bench seats attached to both its long sides. There's a chess board on the table with a few chess pieces still on it, and she's standing at the short end of the table staring at them, looking like she's figuring out her next move.

"Hey," Holden says, by way of greeting.

People can see them through the glass doors of the TV room. Lots of patients can.

"Hey, yourself," she says, not looking at him.

Holden stands next to her and studies the board, too.

"—*whoa,*" he says, "how'd you do *that?*" Black queen surrounded by four pawns opposing. "Who's winning?"

"You played chess, you wouldn't ask."

"—no I mean, who are you, black or white?"

"Both."

"—oh," he says, quietly, with some respect. "Whose move?"

"The lady's."

Holden frowns. "Are those pawns, you know, pawns or have they been kinged or—"

Finally she looks at him.

Those peacock blues.

And tells him, "We don't usually talk while we're playing."

"I knew that," he says, trying to inject some humor into this, get her to lighten up a little. "That's why I interrupted. Because we need to talk."

91

She stares at him, takes a step closer.

"Because I think I probably misled you. Earlier. Today. With what I said."

She's standing so close, suddenly about a million things are running through his mind, mostly all about how near her body is to his, but also how clear her eyes look for somebody who's probably on heavy medication.

She touches his hand and there's another spark—her electricity, or theirs, or his—some active *thing* going on between them.

He takes a step back, the bench seat pressing the backs of his legs.

"See," he says, "I don't want you to think we actually know one another. I know I said that—I know I gave that impression—but we don't. I don't want you to think that. We don't know each other, okay? We've never met."

She takes another step forward. He tries to back up but ends up sitting down. She sits down beside him, their bodies touching. "Which?" she says.

"—*what?*"

"We don't know each other. Or we've never met. Which?"

"—'which'?" he repeats, mystified.

"—because sometimes"—she leans her right elbow on the table and looks over her shoulder at him so the patients in the TV room can't see her face—"people come here. People I've never met. People whose faces I've never seen before. People whose faces don't ring a bell. And they say that they know me. They try to get me to play along. But I don't." She takes his hand in hers and says, "That's what I thought you were doing. Except"—she strokes his hand with her thumb—"it really does feel like I know you from somewhere. But—" She looks away, watches the sky for a moment, then tells him, "It feels like I know lots of things from some place else." She shields her eyes from the rays of the setting sun. "Does that happen to you?"

"—sure."

She brightens.

"—it *does*?"

He takes it back. "I mean—maybe not like it happens to you. It's a relative thing."

"A relative thing?"

"—yeah, like if I ask, 'Is the sun too bright for you?' You know? It's relative. To each person's point of view. Like—if I say—how much pain are you in. Do you remember dreams."

"Have you been in love."

"—yeah, like that. Exactly."

"No I mean, have you ever been in love?"

"—me?"

He looks at her.

He tilts his head until her head shades him from the sun. "No, I don't think so," he says. "But you have," he tells her.

He watches the change that starts to come over her. Watches the way that her whole personality seems to leave her expression, leaving her face like a mask.

"Who are you?" she whispers.

"—Holden," he says. "I used to work with Noah."

"—oh my god!" She throws her arms around him. "—you're Holden! —did Noah send you? Where is he?"

"—wait a minute—wait, wait."

He takes her shoulders.

"Are you saying you remember me?"

"—your name—it sounds familiar."

Holden waits, conscious of the fix he's in and the fact he doesn't have a clue what to do next. In front of his eyes she starts to disappear again. Just cuts out—her look a total blank, like a cell without genetic imprint, like a state before naming—a condition, not a search—an acceptance, not a challenge.

He gives her shoulders a shake.

"Melanie—?"

It's like staring at the sky on a clear night—that's what it's like, he thinks—the blankness in her eyes—like an infinity, exposed. Beautiful, but eerie—like a soul exposed in the fixed gaze of some-one dying or in the round unfocused eyes of babies. This is where she goes—somewhere *in there*, inside herself—when she's living with the past, he thinks. And even as he's registering this obvious conclusion, her hand jerks up and starts moving in the air like some kind of spastic zombie ritual in a monster movie. "—oh *fuck*," Holden breathes, looking toward the glass doors for an orderly or someone who can help him here. "—okay—*hey*," he says, shaking her again, trying to focus her attention back on him. But she's writ-ing now. Writing in the air in front of him, and although the greater part of him wants her attention to return to the present moment, part of him wants her to remain wherever her ragged mind has taken her, to that place where her memories still live.

"—hey, listen . . . listen," he says, soothing her, easing his hold on her shoulders, easing his hands over her fingers, holding her hands still in his, lifting her palm to his cheek to keep her hand still, finding her wrist near his lips, feeling her pulse on his mouth. And suddenly the nature of their touch shifts like melting ice, from the prudent to the tender, and he kisses her, kisses her hand to bring her back, let her know she's not alone.

In her eyes, forming slowly as a seed, a tear rises, hanging on her lashes like a lantern before lighting down her cheek, where he stops it with his finger, not surprised it tastes so sweet.

It's like watching somebody coming out of a deep sleep, he notes. Out of a coma. Suddenly—or not so suddenly—gradually, she's *there*.

"The first time I met Noah," he says, wiping away the last tear from her cheek, "I was really scared of him, really intimidated. I thought I was going to—" He stops himself from saying *die* and says, instead, "Break out in sphincters and shit myself unconscious."

She blushes at his language—but she smiles, too.

"The two of you don't look anything alike, you know that?" he says. "Until you smile. Then that John family dazzle kicks in. I mean—in your case the dazzle is there, anyway. Even when there's no smile. You okay now?"

She nods—doesn't let go of his hand.

Holden senses he can hold her attention if he goes on talking about Noah, so he does. "He's pretty terrific, you know. Your brother. I mean, I think he's the best man I've ever met—the most important person to me that I've ever known."

"—me, too," she says.

He squeezes her hand, looks away, his thoughts lingering on Jason, her husband—and her boys. "Oh, Melanie," he sighs.

"Never call me that," she tells him.

He looks at her.

"I'm 'Johnnie' to you."

"—'to me,'" he checks.

"—to everyone. Johnnie's who I am."

She refuels her smile.

"Tell me more about my rotten brother."

"What do you want to know?"

"Where he is, for instance."

"—where he is," Holden repeats. "Where do you think he is?"

"—see? *He* does that!" She gives his arm a playful punch.

"—that's exactly what he does—ask a question, get a question in response. Graham does it, too."

"—'Graham,' " Holden repeats. "—*doctor* Graham?"

She nods.

"Like I'm not a lawyer who recognizes a discovery tactic, knows her voir dire when she sees one. I know exactly what it means when you answer with a question. It means you want to know more than you're willing to reveal. It means you're safeguarding information. Hiding something. Do you play chess?"

"—ah, yeah. Never to win," he finesses.

"Then what's the point of playing?"

"You only play to win?" he guesses.

"I'll show you," she tells him and starts to man the chessboard.

"I, um, kinda hoped you'd tell me more about your brother and yourself."

"—what's to tell? He's a creep. He hasn't called."

"When was the last time you heard from him?"

"He's forgotten all about me. Black or white?"

The board is ready.

She stares at him.

"He doesn't know you're here, Johnnie," Holden tells her slowly.

She rotates the board so his is black, sits down across from him, raises the white queen's knight and prepares her gambit. "—then *tell him*," she tells Holden. "Your move."

HOURS LATER, AFTER DARK, a hospital employee appears at the sliding glass door to the terrace and calls, "Time, now, Miss Johnnie."

Melanie waves a hand at him and says to Holden, "—time to leave the ball. Time to catch your pumpkin."

"—shit, just when I was winning."

"—in your dreams," she says.

He's down two games.

She's a ruthless, concentrated player.

"—rematch tomorrow?" he requests.

"—if you want."

"—I *do* want," he tells her.

He stands up, looks at his watch and is surprised how late it is. He looks skyward as she folds the board and puts the pieces in the box.

"I bet you're the kind of girl who knows the names of all the stars," he says.

"—in Latin," she brags.

On the threshold of the dark TV room they pause, mesmerized by a soundless image on the television in the corner. "—what the hell is that?" Holden marvels.

A written explanation appears across the bottom of the screen, explaining it's a close-up of a locust.

Then there's a still of an "artist's reconstruction" of a plague in Biblical Times with the printed caption STORM OF LOCUSTS IN THE OLD TESTAMENT. Then a library clip of a modern storm of locusts. Then a location shot of hailstorms falling.

"—oh, hey," Holden says, "I saw this! I was there! This is the hailstorm from this afternoon. Why's the sound turned off?"

Melanie is standing slightly behind him on his left side and he doesn't bother to turn around and look at her for an answer.

"When the sound is on, some of the people here talk back to it," she tells him.

He can feel her move in closer to him.

"—this must be the Late News," he says, because now they're showing clips from the Senate Waco Hearings and there's a shot of Attorney General Janet Reno giving testimony. Holden turns his head and says, "—do you know who that is?" Melanie shakes her head. As she does so he feels her hand at the small of his back. He feels a warmth run up his spine. Then between his shoulder blades he feels her drawing something. A shape. No. A letter.

She's writing.

He stands totally still, pretending to watch the TV, his every nerve alert, until she finishes the final letter.

The imprint of her touch against his body blazes yellow phosphorescence in his brain the way the image of bright light imprints itself on your eyelids when you close them.

Holden closes his eyes and reads,

ꓔ Ǝ ꓠ A ꓩ
O ꓠ Ǝ ꓤ

He turns around to look at her, his breathing trapped somewhere in his throat, and sees that she's gone blank again.

That absent stare.

He takes her hand and says, "Walk me out."

She follows him.

At the desk there's a new nurse, The Night Nurse, who keeps a beady eye on them.

"—bye," he tells her at the door. He lifts her chin so she will focus on him. "I'll come back tomorrow."

He steps away, pushes the door open.

"—Holden!" she cries.

Before he turns the full way back she throws her arms around his neck and presses both her lips against his cheek so the nurse will think she's kissing him but instead she whispers

get me out of here.

THAT NIGHT HE GOES LOOKING FOR LOVE not on the streets of Richmond, not in its bars and clubs or the saloon across the street from his hotel or in the hotel lobby or on the pay-for-play sex channel in his hotel room, but in the top drawer of the nightstand by his bed because he's haunted and he's restless so he pulls out the Gideon. And he goes looking. For Love. For the word. For the first time that it's mentioned. In the Bible. Starting with Genesis.

And how long it takes before you find it might astonish you.

The next morning he draws up the list of questions.

As if he is going to interview Pol Pot or Qaddafi or someone whose every itch and whim have moral implications.

Unlike Chirac, for instance.

Or Bill Clinton or John Major.

From whom there are no vital and exciting answers so why try to ask them vital questions.

But where good and evil are involved you want to err on Good's side so you go prepared. With questions. One. A.

Is there any reason to believe she's suicidal.

B.

Or in any other way a danger to herself.

Two.

What are (is) the legal bases (basis) for her hospitalization.

Three. A.

Has she been judged mentally incapable of caring for herself.

B.

If so, how.

What's to prevent her from leaving voluntarily.

What's to prevent others from releasing her.

What is the worst thing that could happen to her.

Does she have the legal right to know the truth. There are other things he wants to know, too—like how fast can you buy a car—a getaway car—and get all the paperwork done so it's legal in the state of Virginia—but he doesn't write these down. Instead he asks the neighbor, Mrs. Wallace.

"Oh, Paul could let you have one this same afternoon," she advises him. "If everything's in order." Holden's watching her load the dishwasher in her kitchen. "Paul's my husband. He's a Datsun dealer. I bet you're comparin my way of keepin house to hers."

"—to tell the truth, ma'am, no. I'm not."

She spills some washing powder on the floor and just leaves it. "I used to call her Wanda Circle's own little Martha Stewart," she tells Holden, raising an eyebrow. "The Supermom."

"Is that why you won't let anyone clean up the mess in Johnnie's kitchen?"

"—who's Johnnie?"

Holden blinks.

"—sorry, I mean Melanie. I thought Johnnie was her nickname."

"'Johnnie'? Not likely. That house wasn't wantin for more boys' names. Tell me again why you want to use my deck jack?"

"Because it's the closest to the upstairs window. And my wire's only twenty yards long."

"—well is this gonna tie my phone line up? I can't have my phone tied up."

"Fifteen minutes at the most, I promise."

She reluctantly gives Holden the key to the house next door. "You're on your own over there today, 'cause I got all this housework."

"If I didn't know better, Mrs. Wallace, I'd say you're acting a little peeved with me this morning."

"Well I am. I am peeved," she says, scrubbing at her countertop. "—not with you, just with . . . all . . . this. The mess it's made. It's not supposed to be this way. It's not. It isn't fair. You work hard and save enough to get a house in a nice neighborhood and you raise your kids the best you can, you keep them outta trouble and what happens, blam. Something comes along and wipes it out and takes it all away from you. To my mind that's unacceptable. That is just not part of the contract."

"—'contract'?"

"What you're supposed to get. What you expect from life."

Holden starts to tell her something but then stops himself. What's the point, he thinks. He doesn't want to argue with her nor does he believe in her case he could produce her an epiphany. The cost of disappointment is a price without an index, haggled over soul by soul, every body losing something in the bargain. If this woman couldn't cope it's not any of his business. He has his own set of insufficient facts and lousy arguments keeping him from peace of mind. From the pursuit of happiness. Or a house in a nice neighborhood. It's this woman's own stupid fault for believing all that crap in the first place. For believing in the advertising. For reconstructing fairytales instead of footholds on a slippery truth. All you can expect from life is the unexpected, lady, he's about to tell her. The only thing you get with any luck is a chance to wrestle with it when it hits you and pray it doesn't kill you first. But instead of telling her all that he stares at her linoleum and says, "Well I'm sorry Mrs. Wallace."

"—oh well," she shrugs. "'What goes around comes around,' I always say . . ."

"—yeah."

He starts for the door, but stops and says, "—what, exactly, is the thing going around?"

"Oh, the ring," she says. "You know. The gold one. On the merry-go-round."

"Of course it is," he says.

And smiles a cheesy smile.

IT'S DIFFERENT THIS TIME AROUND because he knows her now. He's seen the way her mind works: engaged in chess; disengaged without warning. This time around he feels her presence everywhere, in every room—a captive presence, yearning—and it spooks him. During the night he remembered he'd failed to check the other answering machine, the one in Jason's office—so that's his first stop. But first he fingers the blue satin ribbon on her straw hat.

Something of a perfectionist this Jason, Holden concludes from the look of his drafting table. Most carpenters are.

While he plays back the messages he picks over the items on the table and reads the realtor's advertisement for the house that's framed and hanging on the wall. Melanie must have had it done for him in commemoration—or someone had, maybe not her, now that he looks at it closely it isn't her style, it's a little too tacky, maybe a colleague had done it, or the guys on the crew, his fellow builders, the ones who had turned the blue lines on blue paper from being a blueprint into being a house. Guys like this one for example, Dale—*Jason this is Dale man where are you man I'm out here at the site waitin for the truck man*—or Pete or Fraz (*Fraz?*) or Cully. But no Noah.

He goes upstairs, moving quickly past her bedroom. The room that the computer's in has a double window in its far wall which looks out on the Wallace house next door. All Holden has to do is feed the telephone extension cable he'd picked up through one of the windows, connect the computer to the phone line on the Wallaces' deck and voilà, e-mail. He hopes.

First he has to open a window which, as a result of days of humidity, seems to be stuck. Won't budge. What his fate always seems to have in store for him—a problem better suited to the skills of Arnold Schwarzenegger. He could break a pane. While he considers the pitfalls of pane breaking (possibly none?) he runs his hands up the sides of the window, over its transom, feeling for a hidden lock, and finds instead the window jammed along the top of its runners with several wads of cellophane. They're little bags, self-sealing kind, like the ones that jewelers use for individual gems. These are filled with cut-up weeds and pods.

Holden opens one and sniffs. "—ah geez, kid," he breathes. He looks around the room, overcome with sudden sadness. How old was this kid—Thaddeus, right?—what was he doing with dope at his age? Holden tosses it into a trash can, then changes his mind. He opens the window—it slides easily now—and empties the bags onto the roof. Then he tosses one end of the cable out, plugs the other end into the computer, turns the computer on to get the system going, goes downstairs and outside, retrieves the end of the cable from the yard, carries it over to the Wallaces', plugs it in, goes back upstairs, sits down on Thaddeus's chair, positions the cursor on GET MAIL, takes a breath and double clicks. *Only connect*, he prays aloud—and it does. *You have eight new messages.* Double click. This thing about e-mail—it gets him—the way each one has to have its own title.

HEY DUDE from FERDIE.

Two in a row from some org. in NZ (New Zealand? Let's see . . .) about a volcano watch. Hey this kid is cool, Holden thinks.

A horny little misuse of the information superhighway under MYSTERY MESSAGE from X-RATED . . . and four messages within the last two weeks, titled ONE O THREE through ONE O SIX from someone or something called GASH GIRL. "Dear Thaddeus," the first one starts and all Holden has to do is read the first two sentences before his heart starts knocking.

He'd worked side by side with this singular voice for too long not to be able to recognize its robustness, its idiosyncrasies, its cadence and nutty descants, unexpected punctuations.—*hello old friend* he thinks and touches the computer screen, then whispers, "Noah," out loud as if to conjure him. He prints the letters so he can keep them—then finds and prints all previously stored messages from GASH GIRL. (*GASH* GIRL? he thinks: what the hell is *that* about?). He starts to type:

> Dear G.G.—Holden here. I am sitting in Thaddeus's room at his computer where I've just read 103 etc. Need to speak. Extremely urgent. Am at Omni Richmond. Or contact Dr. Alex Graham Medical College of Virginia.

He thinks for a minute.

Horrible tragedy

he types, then deletes it.
—fucksake you're a writer he thinks just get on with it.
Jason and kids killed he types, then deletes it.
Re-types,

Tragedy here. Need your help.

Sends it, prints it, then erases it from memory. Shuts down
the computer, unplugs it from Mrs. Wallace's line, plugging in the
phone by Thaddeus's bed instead and calls Dr. Graham. He stares
at Thaddeus's pillow, then closes his eyes while he waits.

"—mornin', Holden," comes the now familiar deep voice, "I
understand you partook of some of the delights of my establishment last night. I could tell on meetin you you were a chess playing man."

"I've found Noah John."

"Good lord—that was quick."

"—I mean I found his cyberself. I've sent him an e-mail
telling him to contact either you or me ASAP. Thought I better
tell you."

"—well let's hope we hear from him."

"Oh we will—are you around this afternoon? I have a list of
questions I'd like to ask you."

"—a list! Is this a test?"

"No sir. Sorry. That sounded too stiff. What I mean is—I
have a lot of questions and I'd like to talk to you."

"Not today, Holden, I'm one foot out the door to make a
speech in Roanoke—how about first thing in the morning?—
eight o'clock?—up here in my office."

"—sure. —um, Alex, I'm actually in the house now, in her house, and I was wondering if you think it would be okay to pick up some personal, um, some of her . . . things. Mementos. Some clothes."

"Did she ask you to?"

"No sir. She asked me to do something for her but it wasn't that."

"Well I think everyone concerned with Melanie has got to do whatever's in their power for her peace of mind. I wouldn't go placin pictures of her children in front of her but if you see something there that seems fitting for you to give her to put in her room here—go for it. We're flyin by our seats here, Holden, anyway. So I can't see what we have to lose." He hesitates, gives a little laugh. "—but don't take this as my stamp of approval on your rootin through her closet, son."

No, sir, I won't, Holden thinks.

He unplugs the phone, tosses the cable down into the yard from the bedroom window and shuts it.

The house grows very quiet.

Oh this is weird, he feels.

He stands in each one of their rooms a long time, taking his time. Stands till he feels he's stood long enough. Like visiting a grave.

Then he goes into her bedroom.

It's easy to tell which side of the bed is hers—Jason's has a picture of her and the boys; hers has a picture of Jason.

He picks it up.

Jason the way he must have looked when they met—Jason smiling, dark eyes full of love, obviously looking at her. Long lanky guy with broad shoulders. Muscled arms, gentle hands. Heart drawn in the lower right corner. Written inside it:

J + J

Johnnie & Jason, Holden thinks.

He puts down the picture, goes over to the fireplace and re-inspects the carved rocking chairs. There, on the back of one, on the other side of the same piece of wood the word *Eternity* is carved in, Jason had carved his own name. And on the back of the other one, he'd carved *JOHNNIE*.

His nickname for her.

His, Holden suspects.

His love name for her.

Before their kids were born.

What he called her when they were alone.

In this room.

When they were fucking.

Holden opens some drawers.

One drawer at a time.

Two drawers at once.

He stands in their closet.

Doors and more doors—a carpenter's closet. A closet with closets. A closet for sweaters, lined with cedar. Closet for sheets. One for towels. Closet with shoe trees. Closet with shelves for his shirts. For her shirts.

For the notebooks.

The notebooks—there must be a hundred of them—each one identical—marbled-board cover, pale blue unlined paper, tissue-weight. Lavender scent.

His hand shakes as he reaches for one, choosing at random—the dates on a gold-bordered label on front.

Then the actual sight of her handwriting—not in the air—but on paper.

He takes another one down, careful not to disturb the order they're in.

Holy fuck, he realizes.

From the day she had met him, met Jason, it would seem, she'd been writing their life onto these pages. All through the years of their love, their first passion, their courtship, their marriage—her first failed attempts to conceive—everything, every newness, the weather, the phase of the moon, days' events, each birth of each son, each exploration, first step, first heartache, was here, in these books, on these pages.

This is like—who was that guy? Holden tries to remember, his mind doing cartwheels—this is like that guy in the Pyramid in the dark finding Tut, like that guy who found Troy, like finding a goldmine, like walking into a closet and into Fort Knox or into an archive—

This is like Saint Peter's reading list on his lectern in Heaven.

This is your life, Holden knows.

WHAT'S THE DIFFERENCE BETWEEN BEING A VOYEUR AND BEING A REPORTER?

Funny you should ask.

Because the last thing you want as a journalist is someone watching you. Someone on your trail.

When he gets back to the Omni from Wanda Circle around one o'clock that afternoon the doorman tells him, "There's a woman here asking for you."

At the reception desk he's told, "There's a woman asking for you, Mr. Garfield. She's in the café."

Funny how it happens when you're looking for one person in particular you look straight past another that you know.

"—*Holden?* Is that you?"

"—*mom!*"

"—I couldn't wait!"

Holden lifts his mother in a hug.

"—mom, jesus. Kanga, look at you. You look great."

She's thinner now than when he'd seen her last—altogether trimmer.

"—you're doing something different with your hair," he poses.

"—*you* should talk!"

"—I mean I can't get over it—you look really different. You haven't had cosmetic surgery, have you?" he jokes.

"—no! but god you know who has—?"

"Sydney."

"—how do you know?"

"—how did they look?"

"—terrible! I couldn't stop staring at them—what a botched job! She doesn't have the build for them, you know, she was such a fine-looking flat-chested girl . . ."

"—come on," he says, "let's go have a ridiculously expensive lunch."

She pulls a *Washington Post* from her oversized tote bag and hands it to him. "You might not feel like eating once you've read this."

Holden stares at it—it's the obituary page. "—somebody we know has died?"

She points to the births column.

"—yesterday's paper," she says. "No one even told me he was pregnant."

Holden reads the announcement:

Born to Mrs. Raine ("Sunny") Day Garfield and Mr.
Peter Garfield, White House Advisor, of Georgetown,
a son TURIN on the 6th of August at National
Children's Hospital, five pounds, six ounces.

"He must have been a premie from the looks of it," Kanga
observes.

Holden shakes his head. "Jesus fucking H. Christ," he murmurs. "He might have had the decency to warn us. What does the
son of a bitch think he's doing?"

"Probably he thinks he's starting over," Kanga says.

"—like he did such a great job the first time."

"Well he did—didn't he? Look at you, you've turned out a
treat. Give him some credit. He's your father, dear."

No he's not. Any expectations I might have had about what a
father is or should be were disappointed by this man a long time
ago. Like Sydney said: when your father dies you're on your own.
When your father is dead you father yourself. You out live your
need for a father.

"Anger is bad for the soul," Kanga tells him. "Let it go."

"I already have," he pretends.

IF YOU CAN MAKE YOURSELF FORGET your father then
you can make yourself forget your child. Or you can make yourself remember.

They're standing in what has to be the most macabre exhibi-
tion he's ever seen—including that snake place in New Mexico
and the Museum of Flagellation in Spain.

This one's called, of all things, *Women in Mourning*.

It's about the way mourning became a social virtue after the

Civil War, just in time for the vogue sweeping through England under the widowed Queen Victoria, and there's no one to blame for what he's doing in such a weird place but himself.

In the wake of reading the *Post* announcement and learning that he has a brother, of all things, Holden didn't feel like facing food so he and Kanga decided to splash-out on dinner instead, working up appetites by taking in Richmond's sights.

And since the hospital is smack-dab in the Capitol region, in the historic district, Holden makes a quick stop to see Melanie. Because he promised.

He takes her her hat. The one with the blue ribbon.

"What's this for?" she asks, frowning.

"To keep the sun from your eyes—relatively."

She doesn't recognize it.

"—listen," he says. He touches her chin. "I can't stay right now. But I've got a lot of important things to tell you. I'm coming back tomorrow to see Dr. Graham, so I can see you then. The really important thing you need to know right now is that Noah hasn't forgotten you. Are you listening to me? I've done what you asked me to do. I've been in touch with Noah." He takes her hand. "And you're not alone. I'm here to help you. And very soon, Noah will be with you, too. Okay?"

"—so no chess, then?"

"Did you hear what I was saying, Johnnie?"

She stares at him.

"—I gotta go," he says, squeezing her hand.

"—*why?*"

"—my mom's downstairs."

She blinks.

"—you have a mother?"

Holden laughs.

"—yeah, of course I do. Everybody does."

"I didn't," she says.

He swallows hard, the way she's looking at him.

"Johnnie, I have to go—I haven't seen my mom in like a million years. I'll be back tomorrow. And we'll talk some more. Okay? I promise."

Her hand flies to her sternum and she takes a breath and parts her lips again in that way he's seen a few times now as if she's about to slip back into her inner timelessness but this time she takes a full step forward, this time the spark spreads its electric field from his toes to his ponytail as she puts her arms around his neck and kisses him as if her body needed his in order to survive.

SO IT COMES TO THIS, he reasons:

If God;

then, Eternity.

And if not God, then only living memory.

He and Kanga are standing at the entrance to the gallery called "Life and Death—Mourning in the Old South and the Confederacy," looking at bombed cities and dead babies.

Oh great, he thinks. A perfect day out with Mom. What am I doing here? he wonders. Across one wall very nearly life-size is a large reproduction of a photograph called *Burnt District, Women in Black, Richmond, 1865.*

It's a picture like many others he's seen before of people in shadows of ruined buildings, picking through the devastated street scene for—for what? food? wood? traces of existence? loot? a memory?

It might be Dresden, might be the Acropolis, might be Sarajevo. This time it's Richmond.

A four-story building-front commands the landscape like a beached behemoth, sea-bleached to the bone by tides, its windows, doors and roof evaporized, transported in the conflagration back into the earthly elements from which they rose.

In front of it, miniaturized by the random insignificance of their survival, stand three indecipherable male figures in pants.

To the left of them is a cast-iron gas streetlight in perfect order, except its glass globe has been blown to smithereens.

On the right, caught by the camera in mid-flight like enormous eagles caught by a sudden updraft, two or possibly three black-veiled black-skirted figures, *women* bearing their ridiculous mourning attire through the gutted city like a mirage of migratory tents marching through a desert.

And on the left, riveting Holden's gaze, a single bearded man who happened to walk by too quickly to be rendered corporeal by the camera's lens—transparent, like the ghost he has become.

In display cases placed around the gallery there are elements of mourning gear on show—lockets made from human hair, jet jewelry, black silk parasols, black muslin fans—and three headless female mannequins with oddly shaped formidable pouter-pigeon chests in the three stages of established mourning dress: heavy-, full- and half-.

No equivalent exists in modern industrialized societies of the extremes to which nineteenth-century mourners went to demonstrate their grief, their open dedication to the memory of the deceased. Socially ambitious persons in cities such as Richmond, Baltimore and Savannah (to say nothing of London, Liverpool and Glasgow) seemed to evidence as great a fear as any living souls before them had of dying—but what they seemed to fear as much or more than death, itself, was the un-remembered death, an off-stage one. Dying *forgotten* was, for them, worse than simply dying—an entire industry sprang up around the accoutrements of showing to the public that one had gone out with a real big bang.

That one was missed. That one was forgotten. From the corpse a balm of virtual virtue oozed—the act of mourning, mourning *well*, became a middle class gymkhana. To play it, and to excel at it, you had to alter your appearance, send the signal to the world at large that you had entered play and were well and truly outside the general fray of everyday experience.

You had to change your social status through your dress—"you" meaning "*she.*"

She, regardless of her age (even female toddlers), entered "heavy" mourning for—*how do I love thee: let me count the days*—two and a half years during which she covered herself head to toe, including hairpins, stockings and all intimate apparel, in black, like a miner at the coal face, obscuring her own face from public view with a heavy full-length veil whenever or if ever *she* left the funerary confines of home.

A year, at least, of full mourning followed. Half-mourning followed that, for life—in shades of greys and lavenders.

The three mannequins in front of him, each displaying one of the three shades of mourning in a chorus line of decreasing dirge-ness, end with a fourth figure, set apart upon a platform, made to look bizarrely pregnant while in mourning dress, and an eerie frisson of recognition passes through him as he realizes he's looking at the personal effects of Herself, the Ur-widow, the afore-mentioned Mrs. Jefferson (Varina) Davis.

On display is a chart attempting to decode the overlapping periods of her personal mourning. When her son died suddenly she was still in full-mourning for her father, so she had to revert back to heavy-mourning while still displaying traces of the full-.

Her maternity dress on display here was of a fabric appropriate to half-mourning—proof, Holden supposes, that the rigors of grief did not inhibit the relief of coitus.

Among the items of Varina's on display in an adjoining case is a letter she wrote to a fellow widow in 1893, four years after Jefferson Davis's death.

"It does not devolve upon many women," Holden reads in her peculiarly square and rustic hand, "to twice bury a husband and four children, and I am overcome by the memories of the past."

Holden blinks.

—*twice bury?* he thinks and reads through it again before he realizes that that means they must have dug him up. It hadn't been enough for them, a mourning people stripped of their nation and degraded, it hadn't been enough, their mourning hadn't, to bury their symbolic father once, they had to dig his bones out of the ground in Louisiana four years later and bury them again, in Richmond, replay all their grief, carting out the by-now sick and tired stalwart widow, their Cassandra, in her mothy widow's rags with crinoline stays of worn-out rubbery gutta-percha proving yet again about the deaths of kings that mourning does become the electorate.

"—jesus," Holden whispers to his mom, "they buried this poor fucker *twice* . . ." He shakes his head. "—in Yugoslavia they bombed *cemeteries*. I mean—the cemeteries for godsake. And I never understood it. I thought, What kind of insanity is that? Why bomb the dead? —you know? Why desecrate a grave? Now I think I understand."

Kanga scrutinizes him, concerned by something in his voice, something he's not saying.

"I'm sorry, dear—quite right," she says. "Let's get out of here. That's the problem with the South—they still behave as if the

dust

War Between the States was yesterday. That must be especially
upsetting for you. To be reminded of a war right after you've just
come back from one." She eyes him even more closely, the way
he's staring at the "pregnant" mannequin. "Or are you still upset
about the baby?"

Holden turns on her and says, "—*what?*" too loudly.

People start to stare.

Kanga leans toward him and whispers, "You're very on edge,
Holden, and I don't know whether it's the result of that hospital
visit you just *had* to make an hour ago, or if it's post-traumatic
stress disorder or the start of something else, which I strongly
suspect. *Sibling rivalry.*"

"—fucking hell, mother, can we try and have *one* goddamn
conversation that's not about your former husband? —bury it, for
fuck sake," Holden tells her. "Forget about the bastard and get on
with your life—"

"I *have* gotten on with life," Kanga reminds him, pulling herself up.

They are creating what The South might call some *dust*.

They are quarreling in public.

"—sorry, Mom," Holden concedes.

"—oh, I don't mind," she tells him, taking his arm. "You can
yell at me till hell freezes, you know that. That's what I'm here
for. But you can never fool me, just remember that."

Holden pauses on their way out, holding the door open for
her. "Fool you about what?" he asks.

She throws him a look, and—a little scarily—for the first
time in his life he sees shades of his own face in hers.

"—you *know*," she says, loading it with meaning. "I've been
around men long enough to know why they get grumpy—and I'm
not talking about your father. I'm talking about men, in general."

Holden squints at her in the milky August haze and says, "I'm not grumpy."

"No, of course you aren't, sweetheart." She slips on her sunglasses. "And the tooth fairy lives on a star and the South won the war."

SO IS *EVERYTHING* SIMPLY the result of something else?

How could that be? he wonders.

Nahhhh, that *can't* be, he concludes.

He's driving with one eye open, one eye closed to get back to the Omni long after midnight. Otherwise, oncoming headlights are double.

'Cause if that were true, he continues down that single line of thought, as the alcohol-impaired are wont to do, Time would have no starting point. No alpha. No mother-of-all-mothers. Mother of events.

But if it *was* true, he revises, saying to himself *traffic light up there*, if everything in life is either causal or derivative, then why is he so drunk? I mean, he thinks, did I drink that much for a reason? Why did I allow myself to ply my mother with champagne all night and, in the process, get this shitfaced?

Unless, he recognizes, slowing his speed down *very* subtly so nobody will notice he's way over the limit.

Unless it's elementary, my dear Watson.

Drowning the ol' sorrows, son.

Not having your proper share of sex.

In fact. Not having none.

Okay?

That's it, then. As usual, the Kanga's right.

Just need a proper girlfriend. That's all.

time kid

Nothing whatsoever to do with starting to be turned on by your best friend's sister.

Who just happens to be almost old enough to be your mother.

And is completely whacko.

Nope.

And *also?*

That goddamn tooth fairy *does* live up there. Wherever. On that star.

HE REMEMBERS THE PHONE RINGING and driving, counting three more blocks now two more blocks now one more block getting back to the hotel and the phone ringing setting the alarm clock *ha* you thought I'd forget I have a meeting with Dr. Graham at eight o'clock this morning and why is the light still on, it's grey out there, your phone is ringing.

"—*helmpff?*"

Sorry about the time kid but you said it was urgent.

"—Noah?"

First rule about Bad News, Holden, is you give it straight and fast.

O fuck, Holden thinks.

He sits up, squeezes his eyes closed, tries to obliterate everything around him except the sound of Noah's breathing on the line. I don't know how to say this, he begins.

Sure you do. Just say it, Noah tells him.

Jason, Holden states. And the boys.

There is a real long silence.

Then Noah says, Say that again.

So Holden does.

When? Noah says.

118

June twenty-seventh.

Melanie?

Not in the car. But she must have seen it happen.

Give me a few minutes Holden.

—sure.

You sit there—wherever "there" is: where you are—while in your mind you go and stand beside your friend. He must be calling from a public phone booth, Holden senses, because he can hear the hinged door open, hear the sound of footsteps over gravel through a kind of quiet that communicates an open sky. A bird. Dog barking, or a coyote, maybe. This is that point of relativity, he knows, where people in these situations always swear Time stops. Time slows down. This malfunction of perception, automatic reflex of the brain in the face of crisis. I don't want to remember this, he tells himself, even as he realizes he will. I don't even want to be here now but I know I'll always be here, captive to the memory of this pattern on the carpet, this arc of light, this PLEASE DO NOT DISTURB sign hanging on the handle of the door. Who was it that used to kill the messengers, execute the bearers of bad news? Was it the Greeks? The Romans? Merciful philosophy. Free the bastards from this misery.

I'm going to have to call you back, comes Noah's ruined voice. No use my keeping you hanging on while I, while I try to fathom this.

Holden squints to see the time. "Well, um, aside from finding you to break the news," he says, "there's something else. Melanie . . . she's in a hospital here. They say it's some kind of hysterical amnesia. The doctor needs to talk to you real bad. I've got an eight o'clock appointment with him. Dr. Graham—I already left his number for you. Why don't you call me there, say, eight-fifteen?"

119

the sifting sand

"Is she . . . what do you mean 'hysterical amnesia'? Does she know who she is?"

"—yeah, kinda. She remembers you. But not much else. And she's writing. You know. Backwards. In the air. Like after your mom died. And . . . now she's calling herself 'Johnnie'—did anybody ever call her that?"

"—no, not that I know. But I've been away so long, I don't really know too much about her daily life . . ."

Holden hears him start to break down. "I'll call at eight-fifteen," he manages to say. "—and Holden? How did you get there?"

I'm not really sure.

"I volunteered."

But then again, maybe I was taken captive.

WHAT GREATER CAPTOR is there in this relative realm of shared experience than Time, itself, the big blue meanie without whose constant fix we'd all go insane?

No Time, no optimism. No promise of futurity.

No Time, then no nostalgia.

No New Age, no now, no then, no when, no sooner and no later.

But thrust a stick into the sifting sand, you've made yourself a shadow, that first bar.

Two sticks, you're a genius. Two sticks in the sand and you've made yourself a clock. Your prison.

Poor tiny Dr. Graham is inside the big box in the corner trying to get out, pointing with a stick to a board behind him where there's a drawing of a mid-sliced brain inside a human skull with the title TEMPORAL LOBE LABILITY printed under it. Life-sized Dr.

Graham is laid out on the leather sofa in his office in a pair of running shoes, blue plaid boxer shorts, a sleeveless muscle shirt damp with perspiration and a green baseball cap with the white letters AG embroidered on it. In his hand, the ubiquitous remote. And he's smiling at his own performance.

"Lecture I gave yesterday in Roanoke," he explains to Holden without moving.

Holden looks around for somewhere innocent to sit.

"—about?" he asks.

There's a suitcase open on the only chair.

"—anomalous experiences and the workings of the temporal lobe. NDEs—Near Death Experiences—UFO abductions. Shamanic journeys. Men-in-Black encounters. You name the anomaly—I was on a roll. Grof holotropic breathing, astral projections, earthlight-electromagnetic fugues, acid trips, hypnopompic visions, altered states. The kind of alternate reality that would occur if Time ran backwards. Or sideways. Sorry . . ." He sits up. "I've ordered up some breakfast. I've just been for a run. Yogurt all right with you? Damn storm kept me trapped in Roanoke all night."

"How come it storms so much down here?"

"Convection. Mountains on the west half of the state, water on the other. Throw in cold air comin down from Canada up north and hot air comin at us from the Gulf, the month of August, and you got yourself a climate that gets moody. And the weird thing is now some folks from MIT can link these kinds of storms to migraines, to temporal lobe anomalies, my subject yesterday— these so-called UFO sightings and abductions, earthquakes and their associated luminous phenomena, too. Syncretism—that's what they want us to believe. Some kind of über-dreamland, a mind at large that's just sort of . . ."

"—*out there?*" Holden says.

"—well, exactly."

"I'm not sure I even know what a temporal lobe *is.*"

Alex holds up a plastic model of a human brain. Its surface has the color and textural self-consciousness of a Barbie doll.

"It's these two bits," he explains, balancing the brain between his index fingers as if it were a basketball. "'Temporal' because they're here, right behind the temples of the skull—but 'temporal,' too, I like to think as a mnemonic pun, in that 'temporal' can mean of or pertaining to or limited by Time—short-lived, say— and it's from these 'temporal' lobes that we get the weirdest anomalies, the greatest distortions of time and space and what we call reality."

"—that stuff that you were listing."

"—to name a few."

"—UFO abductions?"

"—oh sure. Various first-person accounts of so-called alien abductions and related anomalous experiences contain a number of common details, repeating patterns, you know, being captured while in a horizontal position, levitating through the ceiling or leaving one's body below—anal/genital probes . . . the incidents, *co*-incidence of which, ufologists will maintain lend a weight of irrefutability to the experiences. But they're asking the wrong question. The right question isn't, How come so many people from so many different backgrounds repeat identical scenarios, report similar phenomena? The *right* question is, Is there a specific area of the brain that, when over-stimulated or mis-firing, induces (a) a feeling of levitation or floating or flying, or all three—*and* (b) anal/genital stimulation which may be interpreted as a 'probe'? And the answer is, Yes. There is. There is a part of the brain that, when malfunctioning, will simulate those quasi-realities. The temporal lobes. They're beauties, son. You could spend a couple lifetimes trying to get your head around their functions. Chiefly they seem to govern not only visual memories but also—with this little button here, the amygdala—they control the emotional content of memories, our emotional responses to what is remembered. For example, when we remove the amygdalas of Rhesus monkeys they don't exhibit general or global amnesias, no, but spookily specific amnesias—they'll remember how to acquire food from a series of trapdoors but they'll forget what species they are, for instance, and try to mate with anything that humps. I had a human case in here once, a woman with an impaired amygdala from a stroke. She could differentiate between parts of her anatomy—tell me correctly which part was called 'face' or 'hand'—but she couldn't remember a specific face. Each time she saw my face was the first time she saw it. Each time she saw *her* face it was the first time. I have a tape here somewhere of a test I did with her looking at her own face in a mirror. Couldn't recognize herself. Couldn't recognize she had a body, that the parts of it that she could name were actually and factually 'inhabited,' animated by her. The 'I' she spoke through was always out-of-body. You know that poem of Auden's that's so popular right now—?"

"—'stop the clocks.'"

"—that one. 'Stop all the clocks' . . . that's what the temporal lobes can do. 'Pack up the moon and dismantle the sun . . .'"

"Is that what's happened to Melanie? She's had a stroke?"

"—oh hell, no."

"—then what has this"—Holden takes the model of the brain in his own hands—"got to do with her?"

"Everything. And nothing, maybe. The point is I have to go at this from every angle. Because I'm not making any progress. I

123

might be overlooking something. I have to try to teach myself how to recognize which questions are the right questions to ask."

"Well maybe I've got something that can help you," Holden says. "Two things. First, Noah's going to call here in twenty minutes. I spoke to him last night. And second—look at this."

He hands Alex one of the notebooks.

"There's about a hundred of these," Holden says. "In a closet. In her bedroom. At the house."

Alex looks back up at him.

"This is what she's writing," Alex says.

Holden nods. "That's what I thought, too. They're just sitting there. An entire intact record of her family."

Alex sits down at his desk, enthralled with what he reads.

"—there's something else," Holden mentions.

Alex casts a glance at him.

"I came to see her yesterday," Holden says.

"—yeah, I know."

"—and I think she's coming on to me."

Alex smiles. "I'm not surprised."

"—oh, *thanks.*" Holden blushes.

"She craves intimacy. She's desperate for it."

Holden deflates.

"I should have warned you," Alex says. He tilts his head a little. "Do you have a problem with it?"

"—well, no," Holden lies. "I mean, now that I know it's nothing personal."

"—oh, it's personal all right. And in a way it's healthy for her, too. As long as you don't act on it."

"—oh no. The thought had never crossed my—"

"—*good.*"

Alex tries to hold his gaze, but Holden wavers.

"—and another thing . . ."

"Is this this famous list of questions that you made for me?"

"No, those can wait. I wanted to ask you about the way she switches off. She just cuts out. Her eyes. Like she goes into a trance. There was something that she did the other night. It gave me the creeps. The news was on TV and there was a clip from the Senate Waco Hearings, a close-up of the Attorney General. I asked Melanie if she knew who that person is and while she was shaking her head no she was writing out Janet Reno's name. It was . . . really creepy. And it made me think. Maybe—for some reason—I don't know. Maybe she's faking it."

"She's not faking it."

"How do we know that?"

"Ever been to a funeral, son? One where there's a woman who's just lost a husband or a child?"

Holden nods, remembering the woman who followed him through the village in Yugoslavia.

"Melanie's not feeling any grief. Not any. None. She couldn't fake that."

"But what is she feeling?"

Alex thinks a moment. "Despair, sometimes," he wagers. "You can see it, can't you? Sometimes panic. Other times—I don't know. She closes down her feeling. Which is why she needs to find a source of it. A new source. Maybe even . . . a flirtation."

"She asked me to get her out of here."

"—oh did she now?"

"Yes."

"—and?"

"—and what?"

"—how did you reply?"

"I didn't."

"How *would* you reply?"

The phone rings.

They stare at it a moment before Alex answers.

Holden can tell immediately that it's Noah. He can't begin to count the number of times he's picked up a phone, just like Alex, and started to engage in conversation with a total stranger, wondering idly about the stranger's looks, the stranger's history and personality. What part of the brain does that? he wonders now. Which part of the basketball? How does the brain convince itself so quickly that the disembodied voice it hears is real and not the voice of God, say, or of some android with a paid-up phone card and a program to communicate? Everyone hears at least one voice inside their heads, the voice of "I." Who does Melanie hear? Which "I"? He remembers a theory from college about human brain evolution which said that the left hemisphere of the human brain wasn't wired to the right side in the way we modern humans know it until two thousand years before Christ. So that what we call conscious decisions such as "Don't piss in the wind" or "Don't secede from the Union" might have been "heard" by the brain as an out-of-body exterior/superior command instead of an integrated rational internal resolution. Still a Voice, sure. But not one's own. Maybe God's. Maybe Satan's. Maybe a Martian's. LSD, peyote, 'shrooms—there was an unabridged pharmacopoeia provending alternative somatic realities that he'd never even opened, never tried. People left and right were "suddenly remembering" things that had never happened to them while he's busy trying to forget the things that really had. Others channeled back and forth through time, all he did was channel sideways in the rut of a poor schmuck impaired by the corticospinal limitations of a single life. How many times had he been party to acquaintances slipping into something just a little bit more comfortable, an alternative reality through drugs you name it mostly dope in high school, dope and coke and tranx and drink at Harvard, alcohol and coke at work, alcohol exclusively and in extreme in Yugoslavia— What had Holden done? Where was Holden while their parties channeled on? Mister buttoned down—or up—whichever way the buttons kept control. Mister straight ass that was Holden. If Alex here were to suddenly look up and say, Here—take this, Here's your trip to Heaven, would he take it, even now when he was more fed up with himself than he had ever been?

Suddenly he sees that maybe *that* was where she'd meant when she'd asked him to get her out of "here." Not out of the hospital. Out of hearing range of whatever inner voice or voices she was holding in her head, out of the prison of her mind, out of her "I."

"I wish I could tell you that, Mr. John," Alex is saying, "but mapping the brain—mapping the personality—its like mapping the Universe before the birth of Hubble. Every so-called 'constellation' is a line-of-sight effect. That's why I need your help. To give me some additional graph points. New perspective. The only thing I'm bound to, by my oath, is to try to do your sister no further harm. I'm not bound to cure her—in fact I can't. I can't 'cure' the circumstances life has dealt her. But I can—I must, I will—vouchsafe a quality of life for her that will attempt to keep her away from any further harm. Now that might be through medication, it might be through psychotherapy—I just don't know. But I figure you can help in several ways. First—and most important—you have to come to see her. Relieve her isolation. Let her know she's not alone in what she's going to have to face. Second—in the meantime—tell me what you can about her inner resources, her previous response to crisis. She seems to me to have been quite stable, quite secure, quite motivated and ambitious. Someone surrounded by and capable of giving a great deal of love."

On the word "love" Holden becomes aware that he's been tracing the fissures of the plastic brain with his fingertips and he almost drops it in his rush to put it down, his own brain no doubt revolted by the prospect of examining its likeness.

Not a good thing to be handling on a morning with a hangover.

Or on any other morning for that matter.

"—sure," Alex is saying, and hands Holden the phone.

"Noah," Holden says.

"Do we trust this guy?"

"I think so. Yes. Absolutely."

"—well I've got a situation here," Noah says.

"What kind of situation?"

"—well basically . . . a life."

Fuck, Holden thinks.

"—and I'm going to have to call you back on this."

"—why?" Holden asks.

"Because I just am."

A beat passes. "No problem," Holden finally says. "I'm here for the foreseeable."

"—how come you're not working?"

Holden doesn't answer.

"I forgot to ask," Noah continues. "Is she fit to travel?"

Oh Christ, Holden thinks. This is how he's going to let me know he's not coming. "I'll have to let you know on that one," Holden says. "What kind of, um, destination are we talking?"

"Cross-country."

"So like—?"

"South Dakota."

Holden notices the way Alex is watching him.

"Not real big on neuropsychology facilities out there, are they?" Holden asks.

"Well the place is wall to wall Air Force and military so there must be . . . I'll find out."

"—because we're talking about getting her the best care possible, right? Aren't we? Isn't that the only thing that matters here?"

"Absolutely."

Holden runs his hand over his eyes. She's your sister for christsake, he wants to say, but "Some people never have to choose between two people they love," Noah tells him before he has a chance to speak. "They get a single go at love and it's smooth sailing all their life."

"I don't *know* any of those people, Noah."

"—sure you do. Look in the mirror. Ask around. You may be one. As for me—you know this, kid—I had to make a choice. I didn't want to but it's the choice I had to make to be with who I'm with. No turning back. You understand?"

Holden looks down at the desk, at the pictures of Alex's children.

"—do I understand?" he repeats, conscious of Melanie's opinion of what it means to answer a question with another question. "—the truth? No. No, I don't." He touches a framed portrait of Alex's two daughters. "I mean—I've never had a sister. And—" He's aware of Alex watching him, so he turns his shoulders slightly so his back is facing him before he says, "I've never been in love."

Noah tells him he'll call him at the Omni later that night, and they say goodbye. When Holden turns around to put the phone down, Alex says, "He's not going to help her, is he?"

"No, he's going to help her," Holden tries to emphasize. "He is," he says again, trying to believe it. "He just has to find a way to do it."

Alex stares at him.

"What's the problem?"

"His . . . situation. He's in a situation, with a woman, where he can't afford to let his whereabouts be known. Basically they're— they're underground. I can't say a whole lot more than that."

Alex stands up, looks out the window.

"Well she mustn't know," he says.

"—how can she not know?" Holden says, going over to the window to stand beside him and look out. "Either he comes or he doesn't come—she spends half her day already just waiting for his phone call."

"Well maybe that's all she'll get. Maybe that'll be good enough. Get him to talk to her by phone. What I meant was, she mustn't know he's made that *choice*. I hesitate to think what it might do to her if she even halfway thought she'd lost that one vital connection. Too."

Below them outside at street level, two hospital attendants and a nurse are steering a male patient from the hospital entrance toward a waiting car.

Holden sees the man is overweight, shaky on his pins, still in a hospital gown and sporting an out-of-place baseball cap which he instantly recognizes as belonging to his old heart-arrested friend from the airplane, Orioles. A woman climbs from the driver's seat of the waiting car and runs around the front of it to open the passenger door.

"What would you do?" Alex asks as they watch the scene below.

"—if I were Noah?"

"If you were me."

"Wrong question, sir," Holden tells him.

Below, Orioles shakes free of all assistance and turns to wave to someone hidden from their view back in the entrance.

Just for the fun of it Holden waves too.

"The right question is," Holden says, "what would I do if I were Melanie."

The hospital employees back away from Orioles, and as the woman with him takes his arm to help him to the car Orioles looks up, spots Holden, and as he starts to raise his hand to lift his cap he clutches at his chest, keels over and falls face first into the driveway of the hospital as help comes running and the baseball cap flies out into the traffic in the street, into the blue, a homer.

THE TRANSPORTATION OF THE SOUL BY GRIEF IS SO LIKE LOVE'S CONVEYANCE that the two must certainly be joined like wheels, to one another.

No love, no grief: a cold heart cannot mourn. A cold heart can inflate with anger to pump outrage as a salve on death's bloodthirsty lesions but salvation, as a routine for existence, stalks on love alone. That's why it takes an isolated death and not a massacre to tip the human heart to pour a grief the mass of which dilutes the differentiated salts of individuals to a common sea of mourning, a grief far larger than an ocean, a grief to drown in, float in like an astronaut drifting from a pod through silent weightless space without passing through the actuality of dying.

Grief of that trajectory must shed its tears in points that graph, plot its flight plan, form a profile, shape a face. We are creatures born with faces and we need to hang a face on death to greet it. More grief, then, for the lonesome hero than for all of Hiroshima, more grief for the holy pilgrim than for all the holocausts. Numbers numb. We cannot weep for millions we can only weep by ones. Grief ruminates on crumbs. Therefore what the genocidal lessons show: the more you kill the easier the evil is forgotten. Kill a Congress, not a President. A congregation, not A Jew. An entire nation, not a martyr. The more you kill the less distinctive is remembrance.

For in mourning, less is always more.

If he could hang the memories of all the faceless deaths he'd witnessed, all the voiceless sorrowings on her blind purity, draw their names and dates on her blank slate, allow her to become the one among the multitude whose fates had left him exiled by exclusion, if he could love her and by loving help perform the miracle of grief then he might save himself as well as her. He would never be the great love of her life, he knew that, love of that dimension visits only some and only once. But he could be the love she needed to remember the lasting gifts her greater loves bestowed on her. If she could begin to see a love returned, see love's face in his, recognize her own face in another's, then she might regain the sight of truth in place of shadowy deception.

If she could help him to forget, he could help her to remember. If they could learn to face their grief together, then they would have entered a place, a state, a levitation, a relief, a grace, a condition, a remembrance—almost heaven—where time does not exist, where nothing's ever lost and the experience of loving never makes us mourn.

LIKE WEATHER, you could say: it happened more or less that way, the way that weather happens, like "a sudden shower"— something that rapidly occurs as the result of a long process. Something happens—a twister touches down, a hurricane reverses course—which, in retrospect, should have been foreseen. Nothing "sudden" about it except that it occurs contrary to somebody's estimated time for its arrival. But nothing is what happens in a void. All occurrences observe the laws of nature. All occurrences are causal.

It was going to happen anyway.

So let's just say it didn't start when he put the key in the ignition and turns to her and jokes, "Where to?" Let's say he knew what they were going to do before that moment. Before Noah told him definitely no way was he coming to Virginia. Maybe it even started from the first time that he saw her, from that first electric touch. Still, most occurrences, although causal, are equally cumulative. Not one, but many parts come into play— and when you're looking for the reasons why we are the way we are and why we do the things we do, it's best to stick to science, to the facts, like a good journalist, because all the rest is sleight of hand, hocus-pocus dressed as gospel. Forecasts dressed as futures.

Something the good doctor had alluded to, a casual remark Alex had made, certainly had causal implication. Holden had posed the question, "What would you do if you were Melanie?" right before ol' Orioles went down for the count for a second and what appeared to be a final time, when Alex somewhat absentmindedly observed, Well one thing I *wouldn't* do if I were Melanie is I'd never get in a car again.

Then while they watched people rush a gurney out to Orioles and lift him off the ground and try to regulate his spastic heart, Alex said, "No I take that back . . . if I were Melanie I might get in a car again . . . in fact I might welcome the opportunity. But I would for fucksake never on my life get *out* of one again and that's for sure."

And then he looked at Holden.

"—what kind of a, uh, car were they in when it happened?" Holden had asked.

"One of those people-movers you have to get when you have that many kids—you know, with the sliding doors."

Then Holden asked, "Does anybody know why she wasn't with them in the car when they got hit?"

"Yeah, she does," Alex had said.

"—no I mean do *we* know why she wasn't in the car?"

"—not for sure, no. All we can figure is that she must have been pretty far away, at least fifty, sixty feet, not to have been caught by it. You saw on the tape what she looked like when she came in. Not a scratch on her. They'd obviously stopped to let her get out for whatever reason . . . I don't know . . . maybe she needed a pee, maybe she saw something in that field she wanted, maybe something flew out of the window of the car and they pulled over while she went back to get it—whatever the reason, if they hadn't stopped they might not have been hit. They might have had a chance to outrun it. Either way, if she hadn't gotten out when she did she would have shared whatever fate was going to happen, she would have ended up still with them one way or another."

And maybe that's when Holden knew he'd have to buy a car that she could stay in for however long she needed to without her having to get out again for any reason if he was going to do this thing with her. Not to stretch, or to pee, or to eat, or to wash, and not to sleep.

And that meant: a van.

Used, but fitted with a microwave, two-burner stovetop, fridge, TV, stereo CD, head and shower, bench seats that pulled together to a queen-size bed, two swivel captain's chairs up front, the '89 Dodge van had cost him $12,999, ten of it by cashier's check and the rest on his American Express.

When he'd finished the paperwork with Paul, Mrs. Wallace's Datsun-dealing husband, Holden said he needed to go back to the house on Wanda Circle one more time and Paul gave him the house key from his key ring, telling him to keep it, as if a key to her house came as an extra with the sale.

He drove to Wanda Circle almost by reflex, on autopilot, barely remembering the difficulty he'd had finding it the first time a few days ago. It had started raining, but by the time he drove into her driveway it was steaming where the sun was burning off all traces of the sudden shower.

He let himself in.

Almost lovingly, with great care, he spent an hour cleaning up the kitchen, washing every cup and plate by hand, wiping down the counters till they sparkled. Then he went through the house and chose his items carefully. He had two intents, the first to fit the van out with the things it needed—blankets, pillows, sheets and towels; her brand of soap; CDs; a bucket, shovel, hammer and assorted tools; kitchenware. His other task, the one he'd really come for, was to pack up all the notebooks. He placed them in a camping trunk he found in the garage, locked it with a key he slid behind his driver's license in his wallet, and stowed the trunk under the spare tire in the bottom of the van.

It was seven-thirty by the time he'd had a shower at the Omni back in Richmond and he took one of the notebooks, the one he'd shown to Alex, with him to read. On his way out he told the desk clerk, by now his confidant, where he was going, then walked to the corner and went half a block down Cary to his favorite local burger spot, Sam Miller's Warehouse. Half an hour later he's sitting in a front booth across from the bar nursing his second Sam Adams from the tap, distracted by some documentary on the TV high up in the front corner about how Alcohol, Tobacco and Firearms had fucked up so stupendously before the FBI went in and fucked up even more than ATF had in Waco, when all of a sudden this giant shadow comes out of nowhere and falls over him.

"—hey," Holden says by way of greeting, not at all surprised.

"—mind if—?" the looming figure asks.

"—my pleasure. If you can fit . . ."

The tall man squeezes in, loosens his tie and signals to a passing waitress.

"I can't get over how big you are," she says. "How big are you?"

"—six-six. One six short of Satan," Alex tells her, and Holden's disappointed that she doesn't get it. She starts to hand Alex a menu but he waves it off. "I want a big pot of your sea-steamed shrimp," he says. "I want two ears of grilled corn and I want a plate of sliced tomatoes, nothing on them. I want a Bass ale to start, and I want a bottle of your best mash left here on the table with a shot glass. Please. Two shot glasses. Thank you."

He slips off his tie, undoes his collar button and the waitress turns to Holden. "Five and ten," he says, "like Woolworth's," but she doesn't get that either. "I was going to have a burger but I think I've been outclassed," he adds.

"Bring him the same as me," Alex instructs.

"—with fries," Holden amends.

136

When she leaves, Alex rolls his sleeves up and stares at Holden.

"Are you avoiding me?" he asks.

"—um, you're kinda difficult to avoid when you're sitting thirteen inches from my face."

"I understand you were on my floor with Melanie last night and again this morning."

"Yeah, I was."

The mash arrives with two shot glasses.

"To your health," Alex says. He pours, and knocks one back.

"You're angry," Holden observes.

"No sir I am not," Alex says. "I am not angry. If I were angry I would bar you from my hospital having seen the last of you and never give you a second thought. Instead I'm sitting here in front of you with a quart of corn liquor between us. That's how not angry I am. Hear anything more from the brother?"

His ale arrives and he gives it a second shot of mash to chase.

"—no," Holden lies, knowing Alex will see through it.

They look at one another in the low light in the dark-paneled booth across the narrow polished table dressed with checkered napkins and assorted beer mats while the TV sends out the noise of an armored tank assaulting a religious compound in the background.

Holden takes a sip of the corn liquor which ignites a firecracker in his esophagus.

Alex waits.

The cutlery arrives.

Holden fidgets with it, sips his ale.

"He's trying to find out if there's somewhere she can be that's closer to him," he finally admits.

"And where would that be?" Alex says.

Holden pushes a beer mat in a circle.

"South Dakota," he says.

Alex leans so far across the table Holden feels his breath against his face.

"Do you sincerely want to help this woman or don't you?" he says.

"—of course I do."

"Well, then, son, if you're going to move her—and I pray to God you're not—then you better damn well not go behind my back. You better damn well beg me to cooperate in finding her the care she needs because I'm telling you right now when she blows, and we both know that she's going to, she is going to blow with so much force that it might destroy not only her but also anyone and anything around."

Holden stares at him, unblinking.

"You don't know that for a fact," he says.

"—jesus christ," Alex swears. He runs his hands over his head and slumps back in the booth. "I wish you wouldn't do this," he tells Holden, his anger having ebbed.

"—'do' what?"

"You know damn well 'what.' I don't think you get it, boy. I don't think you understand the danger. You need to tell this so-called brother I'm not in the business of accommodating his love life. Mohammed needs to get his ass in gear because this mountain isn't budging."

Holden lets this ultimatum dissipate a little before saying, "Let's just say there *is* a plan to move her. Let's just say that. Give me one solid scientific reason why that can't be done."

"*You* know damn well I can't."

"—okay, okay, well, then, you're the one who's been insisting Noah's role is crucial—fuck *you're* the one who sent signals all through the universe to find him, now what are you saying? You

138

changed your mind? Because he wants to help but maybe not your way? *She's* the only issue here not whether or not you're going to get another entertaining video attraction on your box-office list of popular case histories—"

"—oh you're accusing me? Let's both lay our ulterior motives on the table, son—"

"—and stop calling me 'son.'"

"Now that you've found the brother, what's in this anymore for you?"

"Bringing them together."

"—and?"

Alex refills their shot glasses.

Holden watches him.

"She intrigues me," Holden says.

"Now that's more like it," Alex says. He lifts his glass to toast.

Holden does the same.

"—she intrigues me too," Alex concurs.

They drink.

This time the mash is sweet and smooth in Holden's throat.

"—but I'm not turned on by what her loss of memory represents," Alex pointedly says.

"What do you mean? —'represents'?"

"Blankness. Innocence. Semblance of the territory of youth. False purity. Come on, you've been around. Why do you think the Playboy bunnies are enduring?"

"Because they fuck like rabbits?" Holden says.

"Why do you think an older man, like your father, trades in his wife for a younger woman?"

"—how do you know about my—?"

"Youth isn't erotic in and of itself," Alex tells him without answering his question. "Hell, youth's too undiscerning to be seriously sexy: it's empty, that's its musk. It offers an illusion that a man can re-invent himself—start clean, start over. It's classic. A classic turn-on. As for your father, it was in the papers. I make a point of reading about other men's affairs. But you were right about one thing—Melanie is one hell of a case history. I don't deny I haven't thought of her as my passport to renown, a chance to do an Oliver Sacks, if not a Freud. Whereas for you, I think there must be an erotic charge to your samaritanism. I think what turns you on about her isn't *her*—wife, mother, woman with a decade of mothering behind her—I think what intrigues you about her is the sexiness of her condition, her absence from history, her non-being, her nullity. Like some kind of symbol for what's really not there. Like a sex symbol or a pin-up."

"You make me sound like a real bastard."

"—no I think you're just . . . a *man*. We all do it. If women knew to what extent we use them to define ourselves they'd rule the playground. They'd take our balls away. Unfortunately for them we've succeeded in convincing them we own ours."

"—oh, so that's all right then. We're all bastards."

A video clip of David Koresh in full messianic performance fills the TV screen as Alex tucks a checkered napkin in his collar and their food is served. He starts going at the shrimp with both his hands. "Name me one cult in the last century that had a female figure at its head," he poses.

Holden frowns, tears a shrimp from its translucent shell and eats it. "What's your point?" he asks, peeling another. "Winnie Mandela. Mary Baker Eddy. Eva Peron . . ."

"Sex," Alex says, wiping his mouth. "As usual. Sex appeal. What makes one person sexy to another. I've got these two daughters, see—Georgia, I told you about, and Holly—and they keep me on my toes. They get me thinking about things from the opposite sex's point of view. For example, this David Koresh phenomenon: why are all today's evangelists male?"

"—because all *yesterday's* evangelists were male."

"No, bear with me. See, they even got me wondering if Melanie's loss of memory might be sex specific."

"Sex specific?" Holden asks.

"I know it's crazy but everything about this case so far has tested all my previous assumptions. It's like what I said a couple days ago—I have to teach myself to ask a different kind of question. Two interesting things happened with my girls since Melanie has been my patient. One was that Georgia's in this summer program for gifted city kids at VCU, and kids in her class had to read a nineteenth-century English novel and Georgia read Mary Shelley's *Frankenstein.* And when it came time for her to give an oral book report she asked me to testify, to be a witness and give evidence—don't ask, it's some new way they have of giving oral book reports, like they're in court before a jury. I think it all developed out of watching Court TV . . . Anyway, she asked me to give expert testimony about the brain transplant, about whether or not Mary Shelley's version of the brain transplant was credible, because—I don't know if you remember this about the novel, I didn't—in the novel Frankenstein comes to life with a blank memory. A total blank. Blanker even than your friend's— than Melanie's. Blank as a baby's. But in the Boris Karloff film version, Frankenstein evidences 'monster' characteristics, which were construed as 'male' thinking—is the brain sexless? Well no, it's not, we know it's not. But is the function of memory sexless? No one's working in that field, yet we're working on studies of differing memory functions between right-handed and left-handed people, for example, but not between sexes. And I think that's frankly troublesome. Very troublesome. Because the other night—this is the second thing I wanted to tell you about that happened with my girls—Holly just out of the blue when I was putting her to bed looks up and asks me Daddy, what's 'forgotten history'? —just like that. 'How come they say women have a "forgotten history" and they don't say the same thing about men?'"

"—bright kid."

"—oh, scary bright. Both of them."

"I bet you're a terrific dad."

Alex sits back. Radiates.

"—I *am*," he says.

"—and your wife?" Holden asks.

"She's not a terrific dad."

"—no, I mean . . ."

Holden senses a shift in the weather. He looks at Alex, remembers the open suitcase on the chair in his office. "—sorry, I don't mean to—"

"—no, it's okay. Listening to myself lecture to you about why some men get turned on I thought, 'What an asshole you are, Alex. What a hypocrite.'"

Holden wipes his chin with the napkin, puts it on the table then holds his hands in front of him, palms out.

On the plates between them is the litter of their meal—husks and shells, the juice and tiny golden seeds of a tomato.

"I don't really like to hear tales of other people's love lives," Holden says.

"I know you don't."

"So spare me."

Alex starts to twist his beer glass back and forth as if it were a lens through which he could bring his thoughts into focus.

"All I'm saying is—I see a little of myself in you, I recognize the signs. Maybe I'm wrong, maybe I'm appropriating your response to Melanie to pacify my own frustration. But my staff sees it, too. I'm not saying I think you're in love with her— maybe you are. But I'm begging you to think of her as someone that you must protect. Can you promise me that—man to man? That no matter what develops, if you do this thing you're contemplating doing, you won't then ever let her out of your sight?"

What a load of retro-sentimental pseudo-macho mildewed crap, Holden thinks. It's what you have to love about the South.

"I'm not her babysitter, Alex," Holden says.

"Tell me what you think you are then."

Holden stares at him.

From the TV come the words "Prophet? Savior? Or a madman?"

Memorable, Holden mouths.

He repeats it. I want to be . . . *memorable.*

Still, even then he isn't completely certain he's going to do it, that it can work, that she will even go along with him, once they leave the hospital. Even when he calls Kanga at six o'clock in the morning and makes it sound like he's going to hit the road like Kerouac, for self-discovery, still he has his doubts. Even when he packs up all his cares and woes and checks out of the Omni.

And, oh good. His favorite god is on the job today. The god that likes to play with thunder, holler at you, Call this rain?! Wait till I give you rain like what I give them in Calcutta!

It's a monsoon out there, but here she sits ramrod straight, waiting for him, eager as a pup, her sunhat tilted back, its ribbon flowing down her neck, her beach bag all packed and ready.

"O geez," he says. "Johnnie. Look at you . . ."

"I'm so excited," she admits, rising to him. "My heart's pounding."

So is mine, he doesn't say.

"—Mr. Garfield?" nurse he's never seen behind the desk before asks him.

She pushes a sheet of paper toward him, saying, "For insurance purposes."

He notices a large manila envelope on the shelf behind her with his name on it. "—is that for me?"

"Dr. Graham said to give that to you when you bring Miss Johnnie back."

"—uh huh. Well is Dr. Graham in right now?"

"He was in and out earlier this mornin."

"—uh huh. Well seeing as I'm here I'll take it now."

She stares at him.

"That Dr. Graham," she remarks. "He said you'd say that." From the desktop in front of her she withdraws another large manila envelope, somewhat larger than the first. "He said *if* you said that—which he must have known you would—then I'm supposed to give you this instead."

She hands it to him.

Holden hefts it. It weighs about a half a pound. On the front of it his name is written in a bold unfussy hand. He opens it. Inside are roughly thirty pages of photocopies paper-clipped together with Alex's business card on which Alex has penned both his home phone and beeper numbers.

The first several pages appear to be copies of Melanie's admission forms and medical insurance information—followed by two dozen pages copied from some kind of professional handbook listing the names, addresses and resident hospitals or clinics of specialists in neuropsychology, state by state. As he leafs through them Holden's hands shake slightly and his throat con-stricts. On each page Alex has drawn a star beside the name of at least one of the physicians, and the states included are, in this order—East to West—Virginia, Kentucky, Missouri, Iowa, Nebraska, South Dakota.

Holden touches his forehead.

Racing back through the pages to the beginning, he sees names of cities blur—Pierre, Sioux Falls, Broken Bow, Lincoln, Omaha, Council Bluffs, St. Louis, Kansas City, Louisville, Bluefield, Roanoke, Lynchburg, Richmond. No star beside the name of Alex Graham.

"—you all right there, Mr. Garfield?" the nurse says.

He looks up at her, nods once. Slides the papers back inside the envelope. Parts his lips as if to tell her something, swallows it instead. Turns to Melanie, who's watching him, standing with her feet together and her hands clasped like a churchlady waiting for amen to signify her silent prayer is over.

He walks toward her and she begins to bounce a little on her toes.

He touches her elbow, their bodies combining in a common warmth, whispers *let's go* and leads her out.

"You two have a nice time now," the nurse calls but neither Melanie nor Holden turns.

At the elevator Melanie leans against him and he puts his arm over her shoulders. They ride down in silence. Through the mus-cles down his forearm he feels her heart race in her chest. In the lobby she slips loose and takes his hand, her fingers cold. At the glass doors she stops and waits for Holden to open them. Then she's under the tiny portico, stopping again, utterly confounded by the downpour.

"—you okay?" he asks.

She turns to face him, tears running on her cheeks.

"—hey—hey," he says, touching her chin, "—we're not going to let it rain on our—"

"—breathe!" she orders, blinking back tears.

"—what?"

"—breathe *in!*" she laughs. "—can't you smell it? Rain! —everything smells sweet!—even the buildings!"

He grins at her.

"—that's your limo over there," he says, pointing toward the van. "Shall we run for it?"

"—you bet!"

They dash the twenty yards through the deluge, Holden fumbling the keys, letting her in the passenger side then running round the back to the other door. In a split second he clocks himself standing where he watched Orioles fall in a heart attack, and before getting in he turns around and looks up at the window through the rain. At who is standing there.

And waves, as Alex steps back from the window.

Then Holden gets in the van with her.

"—this is amazing!" she says. She's balancing between the two bench seats that become the bed, beside the fridge and the stove, behind the driver's chair.

"Do you like it?"

"—I love it! —it has everything! Do you live here?"

She takes the drenched sunhat from her head and, shaking out her hair, tosses it to dry on one of the foam-cushioned bench seats, then retrieves it.

"—Is that a bed? Bad luck to put a hat down on a bed." She crawls into the captain's chair beside the driver's and smiles at Holden, flaxen hair already curling round her face in a lacy aurora, as he knew it would.

Rain falling on the vinyl surface of the van sets up its drumming rhythm while rain falling on the windshield forms an opaque curtain.

"—not much of a road day, huh?" she reckons.

"Are you cold? Do you need a sweater? I can turn the heater on . . ."

She smiles again and shakes her head and says, "No, I'm fine. Everything is perfect."

"—except the weather."

She looks back toward the building, clears the window with her hand. "—it's just good to be out of there." She turns to him and lowers her voice down to a tone he can barely hear beneath the drumming rain. "—they watched me all the time, even when they thought I didn't see them looking, watching somewhere else, through my skin, behind me, never at me. I think they thought I must be someone else." She traces the knuckles of his hand. "But you're different. You're not one of them. It's like when you look at me, you see my soul. Do you know how frightening that is?"

Holden catches a tear on her cheek with his thumb. "Do I frighten you?"

"Oh, *a lot*," she says, smiling. "More than I frighten myself."

This makes her laugh.

"You frighten me, too," he confesses.

He slides his thumb across her wet cheek to her lips, he wants to kiss her.

"*Good*," she breathes.

The inside of the van fills with a dense atmosphere which coats the windows like the inside of an egg. Rain drums.

He turns the key in the ignition, turns the defroster on. Wipes the inside of the window with his hand, looks at her.

"Well," he says, "where to?"

"—to the rotten stinking brother." She smiles, pointing straight ahead.

"To the rotten stinking brother," he repeats.

"—biggest creep in all the world," she adds, wiping down the window.

"—but we love him."

Holden thinks he's never been so happy in his life.

"But you love him," he tells her.

He rolls his window down so he can see the van's rear end in his side mirror and is blasted by a baptism of rain.

She cracks her window and says, "All clear over here."

Holden backs the van out of the parking spot and takes the left on Broad, heading for the Interstate.

Rain comes at them harder as they move. At the first stoplight Holden tells her, "I don't know how far we're going to get today in this, to tell the truth."

"How far do we want to get?"

He throws her a look.

In ideal weather you could drive from MCV on Broad to the first exit ramp off 95 in under ten minutes, but not today. Today weather's like a forgotten memory in the depths of your unconscious. The rain is coming down like a Niagara, militantly. Flood is soil's gravy, the runoff of excess, which occurs when more rain falls than the terrain can swallow, and along with the beds of streams and rivers, paved streets are the first to flood. I-95, a young road compared to Richmond streets, is engineered, at least, for runoff, but Broad is like a water chute in this downpour, brothy with a soapy foam under which the traffic lanes and parking lines disappear like glaucous veins beneath the surface. All water weighs the same, despite its solids in suspension—a gallon weighing eight and a half pounds. One block of Broad, alone, is probably bearing several tons of water in a rain like this, Holden reckons. Your average raindrop isn't much of a ballistic weapon on its own, having sacrificed most of its mass in its fall from heaven, but rain like this one, rain so big it bounces, is more likely hail or snow that's melted in the atmosphere, its more complex formation giving it an added rate of fall of up to eight miles an hour. So rain is pouring on the roof of the van faster than the van is moving forward. And through this wall of water, headlights and traffic signals waver like coronas around distant gassy planets—figures, men and women, seeming not to move at all along the sidewalk, waver in and out of the surrounding scene like living insects caught in amber, stalking the periphery of this restriction as if trapped, not in a lasting condition, but in a fleeting bubble. In the way they walk, head-strong, their postures gauging the wind, they're saying *This is just a cloudburst—I'll just dash across here—This can't last.* It starts, this kind of rain, the way a monsoon starts after the long drought, first with the gift of gentle refreshment, then shifting like a race-car driver on a flat to a speed of rain like pistons firing full throttle. *Surely this will end,* a person from a temperate zone is seasoned to think—but it doesn't end. This is, after all, the rain that's fallen through every human narrative for more than four thousand years: *flood* rain. This is, after all, the rain that's been saving itself like a virgin, teasing us with veiled displays all summer, hoarding drops of the Atlantic like pearls of salty caviar that we could see, not touch, like next year's spawn, a rain on the horizon, next month's rain, tomorrow's. We should be more careful what we wish for when we pray for rain. Both the Bible and Earth Science tell us so—the narratives of India, Babylonia, China, Egypt warn us. Like everything we think

149

we cannot live without, we're the last to understand how radically the sentence of desiring—its season and its penance—can disfigure. Be careful what you wish for, how you wish for it. One man's log raft, one man's ark, is just another's timber pile for burning. On water, as in life, it ain't just wood that floats.

"—*shit,*" Holden finally concedes, "oh *shit.* We can't go on in this. This is insane."

He's been driving at a snail's pace, face close to the windshield, navigating through the flooded lane like a snowplow in a blizzard. Up ahead, flashing lights indicate either an accident or a road closure, he can't make out what the distant hooded figures dressed in yellow are signaling, eerie as a road crew on the moon. With no recourse, Holden pulls off the road under the first overpass for shelter from the torrential onslaught, switches on the hazard lights and looks over at her for the first time since they left the parking lot.

"—Johnnie?"

She's gripping the dashboard, hypnotized, it seems, by the flood in front of them.

He touches her.

The thought crosses his mind that they're in real big trouble.

"—you okay?" he says.

She nods once, quick and sharp, and murmurs, "That was scary."

"—yeah," he agrees. The hazard lights flash around them, reflecting off the wet cement. He rubs her arm. "We'll just stay here awhile till this blows over. Some trip, huh?" he tries to joke, but she doesn't smile.

Nor does this weather smile on them.

For more than half an hour they wait out the storm, Holden making several frail attempts at conversation about the changing patterns in global weather, about global warming, the depletion of the ozone layer, until, as Melanie grows quieter and quieter, he realizes destructive weather, as a topic, is a stupid thing for him to choose to talk about with her. So he tries to think of something else, but can't. Because when you find yourself under such severe circumstances, nothing else seems suitable to talk about.

He turns on the radio and as he fiddles with the dial, a State Police car comes up slowly from behind them and signals them to follow, guides them slowly through the flooded lanes and safely off the Interstate at the first service ramp.

"—now what?" Holden asks himself out loud when the ramp ends in a T-junction. He has no idea where they are.

"Go left," Melanie points.

Holden follows her direction but asks, "Do you recognize this road?"

"Not especially," she shrugs. "It just seems logical that if we're heading west, then—oh good, there's a sign—you got a map?"

"—um, yeah, in the glove compartment, but—"

She's already got it open, and Holden is suddenly panicked that she'll recognize landmarks, the roads she's used to traveling, the name of the town she's used to living in.

"—hey," he says, reaching over clumsily and taking the map from her, "I've got an idea—look over there. Just what we need, right? Just the thing. Just what the—"

"—doctor ordered?" she asks wryly, sending him a look.

The rain, although less dramatic, is still coming down extremely hard, and with great difficulty Holden negotiates a turn across oncoming traffic into the parking lot of a mid-size shopping mall.

"—see? This is great," he tells her. "You're going to love this idea. We can go to Kmart—that'll be fun. We can buy things—

151

stuff we need, you know. Like *raincoats*. And umbrellas. And then we can come over here to Winn-Dixie and do our food shopping, load up with everything we need for our road trip. How does that sound? Doesn't that sound great? And then by the time we come back out, all this Weather will have gone away."

Because she's looking skeptical—or frightened, he can't tell which—before she has a chance to say anything, Holden's out the door on his side of the van, running through the downpour to open the door for her, then leading her, splashing, at a run to the covered sidewalk in front of Kmart, where they're met at the open automatic glass door by a burly managress in a white blouse and crimson skirt and vest who tells them, "Sorry, closed. The electricity is out."

"You're kidding," Holden says, dripping. "All we want is an umbrella."

"—doesn't everybody? Nope, it's out all up and down this side of the highway. And I don't know what I'm going to do about these doors—no way to close 'em."

"But—" Holden starts to say, then notices Melanie has wandered off along the breezeway toward the supermarket, where the lights are still all on. She stops in front of a darkened store selling knick-knacks and assorted junk and seems to be transfixed by her own reflection in its storefront window.

Holden leaves the Kmart lady standing at the open gates of her horde of theft-vulnerable loot and goes after Melanie. She shivers when he puts his arm around her shoulder and leads her to a shopping cart and into the brightly lit wonderworld of the supermarket.

"Okay," he says, keeping up the chatter. He's amazed how many people there are inside the store—as if they'd driven there when the storm began for shelter. Amazed, too, by the set-up of the place—its brightness and its size. You could roll a 747 through here, he considers. You could play baseball. Conduct a mass for thousands. Hold a concert. It had been years since he'd been in one of these, and he was oddly thrilled, a little bit excited by the prospect of so much, so many treats. From the distraction of his own fascination, he doesn't notice Melanie's. Distracted by what seems to be a Matterhorn of fresh-picked corn, he doesn't notice Melanie's attraction to the mirrors canted over the display of misted, vivid produce. As he fills a plastic bag with ears of corn, fills another with succulently ripe tomatoes, he relinquishes his concentration on her somewhat—lets her drift to his periphery—so he doesn't notice right away that she is fixated by what she sees reflected. As he picks his way across a mound of blushing new potatoes, Spanish onions, cucumbers and scallions, he comes close to her again, teasing, "—how 'ya doing? Having fun?" only to be shocked to find her standing there, tilting toward the mirror, fingering the lines on her face, her crow's-feet and laughter's traces, as if she's never noticed them before.

"Johnnie? —hey." He touches her elbow. "I need your help here on the grocery question—"

Slowly she turns to him, eyes completely dull, hands drawn in horror to her face, fingers tugging down the corners of her eyes and just as Holden grapples with the question of whether or not there had been any mirrors in the hospital, whether or not she had seen a reflection of herself, of her face, and wondered how she'd gotten—overnight, mysteriously—so old, how she'd aged without remembering it, where her youth had disappeared to while she wasn't looking, while he's thinking all this, what should arrive, swarmlike, buzzing, teeming down the aisles like mating locusts, but an unanticipated nightmare.

Brownies.

instinct

Little girls in Brownie gear, trained like circus fleas to pull their own on their quest for Brownie badges.

Little girls with lists of things to find.

Little girls with pads and pencils.

Notebooks.

Writing.

Holden's first concern is, "Oh shit, *kids*," and when Melanie starts to follow two of them down the aisle of frozen pizzas and convenience foods with the shopping cart his fear is that she's following maternal instinct.

But she's not.

He hurries toward her.

The two Brownies in the aisle have stopped to comparison-shop frozen french fries, and as they note the prices of the products on their pads, Melanie stocks the shopping cart with five frozen pizzas and five boxes of frozen toaster waffles. Five frozen packages of microwave burritos, pushing the cart along, Holden notes, on a sort of autopilot, five of everything, not "shopping," he sees, in the present—"shopping" in her past, "shopping" from memory, for *them*.

"Johnnie, listen," he starts to say, emptying the cart as fast as she is filling it, in a kind of farce, "we don't really need all this."

He piles her choices back into the freezer bin and wrests control of the shopping cart from her, holding her arm firmly with one hand while he steers toward the deli section with the other.

Next to the deli counter, down the long back wall, there are the meat and dairy sections and several clusters of Brownie two-somes dot the aisles, pricing chopped chuck, butter substitutes and a gazillion kinds of milk. Melanie breaks away from Holden and wanders toward them as he starts to place his order. *Get this over with and get her out of here*, he's thinking. But even as he thinks

154

aw, *fuck it* and toys with the idea of abandoning the cart and making a quick exit, he sees her standing, perfectly calm and, for all appearances, composed in front of a twelve-foot display of discounted cereal. Her hands are folded neatly in front of her as if she's waiting in a receiving line. He smiles at her and she smiles back. He orders a container of fried chicken. He orders ribs. He orders cole slaw. He orders two pounds of sliced Virginia ham. When he turns to look at Melanie again he sees her staring at two Brownies pricing packs of chicken parts. He sees her staring at them writing on their pads. Then, next thing he knows, while he's waiting for his orders to be filled, he feels her warmth beside him, then the shock of her index finger pressing through his damp shirt, etching something down his spine.

Her touch pins him to the spot and he stands stock still, the deli produce swimming in a jellied sheen before him.

He closes his eyes, following her writing in his mind.

It's like looking through the window of his skin, he thinks. He can make out individual phrases, separate words, but as the source of her dictation becomes more fevered, her hand starts to join the words as fast as letters, dropping all the flourishes like a rushed stenographer, losing dots on i's, the crosses of the t's, demeaning its calligraphy to gibberish. After a few moments of these frenzied passes, Holden numbs to the formations like a reptile numbs to scales when it strains to shed them for new skin. She neither looks at him nor speaks, and this mode of behavior, this automatic mode lacks life—like the incessant rain outside, it drums and drums. What she succeeds in communicating has no modulation, no shading of expression, no hope, no doubt. Instead of making eye contact she makes a coded message. Instead of looking at him she forces him to look inside. Instead of serving as the screen in a confessional his skin begins to seal his isolation. He looks at her and whispers *Johnnie* but her mind or her attention, her whole personality, has vacated, moved house. He tries to stop her hand by holding it in his but she pulls away from him when he reaches for her wrist, steps back suddenly as if repulsed by him and goes on writing. Some of the Brownies look around to see what the strange lady's doing.

Holden forcibly restrains her, scooping up his deli packs and maneuvering the cart with one arm at a kamikaze pace toward the checkout counters, dragging her along behind him, murmuring the whole time, like a ham operator lost at sea—come in Greenland, Iceland are you there?—he keeps murmuring, *Johnnie look at me, Johnnie it's okay, Johnnie we're just going over here and out this door.* Truth is he's scared to death. Any number of things could go wrong, he's in waaaay over his head with this one, this isn't just another assignment where he can parachute in, show his credentials, take a quick look around on the ground and leave, relying on events to happen in the way they would without his taking part, relying on the narrative of history to roll on by while he stands on the sidelines, as a witness, and records it. He has a responsibility here. He brought her out into the open, in among a crowd, and now she's acting *predictably*, behaving for all the world to see exactly what she is—a woman with a serious psychological problem. Fuck did he think he was going to accomplish? A miracle? Is he nuts? What was he thinking? She could go berserk at any moment, look at her, he can't tell what she's thinking, can't even tell what planet she is on, her eyes fixed on something only she can see, her goddamn arm going like a band leader's on speed, like Peter Sellers doing Dr. Strangelove from the far side of the grave. At the checkout counter people stare at her, alarmed, and Holden thinks, *That's it, we're going back to the hospital,* as he throws a wad of crumpled bills on the conveyer belt, not waiting for his change.

Somehow, manhandling her impatiently, he gets both Melanie and the cart of groceries through the door, outside, where he makes a mad dash toward the van through the pelting rain.

"*Stay,*" he tells her, fumbling for the keys and cursing, hurling the soaked bags into the van before propelling her toward the door. "Get in," he seethes. He's angry and he's cold. Both of them are drenched through to the skin. But as he takes her roughly by the arm she looks at him and something in her eyes—a flicker— renews his sympathy for her. Her right hand keeps cutting through the air, but in the sallow light of the driving rain he sees what can only be real pain, its spill of terminal despair a miscellanea of scattered sorrows on her face like the debris of a moraine abandoned by retreating glaciers.

And grief is the antithesis of lightning, he sees. It is a dead bolt in the heart—a black arrow, not a blazing one. And something's flickering in her, some desperate signal aimed at him for help. Standing there, rain covering all surfaces in sheets, puddles of it eddying around their feet, ribbons of it flying at them diagonally in the parking lot, he wants to believe the way she's looking at him means the light he sees is a light of something that she's feeling, that she's shining for him only, reflective as his moon. Hope mixed with compassion stirs him as he sees that she would stop this if she could, stop her hand, stopper up its flood of unabridged testimony, abridge its babble, bridge the distance it creates between them if it were up to her, a matter of volition, a clear-cut case of something she could choose. Her look signifies she can't help herself—he sees her anguish, and with a gentle force equal to his emotion, he guides her into the van and closes the door behind her.

When he gets in on the driver's side, she is standing in the back, arms clasped around herself, shivering, the rain on the roof setting up a syncopated rhythm to her excited breathing.

Holden stumbles through the groceries, reaching to a shelf above her for two towels, saying, "Here, dry off, get out of those wet clothes," but when he looks at her he sees she's already ahead of him.

In the dim light of the back of the van the pale skin of her breasts looks opalescent, paler than her stomach and her shoulders, paler than her nipples, a silver rivulet of rainwater running from her collarbone down the center of her sternum toward her navel, twice bisecting her bikini line. He watches, spellbound, as the drop of water sinks into her navel, flattens and changes shape before slipping over that umbilical lip down the vertical plain of her belly to that enigmatic line of stitches between her pelvic bones, the birthing scar.

"Hold me," she whispers.

Holden doesn't move. He's never seen a scar like this—except, of course, *this* one, in the photograph on Noah's desk, years ago. Even then, its shock value mesmerized him. The suggestion of a closed door to a woman's body excited his carnal curiosity. Excited his investigative nature.

Excited, period.

"Hold me," she repeats, *"please."*

She goes toward him, pulling his body against her, and Holden finds himself folding his arms around her shivering shoulders, finding his hands on the skin of her back.

"I'm frightened," she murmurs.

He lifts one hand to the back of her head, consciously aiming to comfort her, while his other hand involuntarily explores the erotic cove of the small of her back.

"I'm afraid," she continues.

"I know," he says, holding her head to his shoulder, smoothing her hair. He holds her more tightly to stop her shaking.

"Something terrible is going to happen," she says. "I know it is. I feel it."

She raises her head up to look at him, her eyes searching his. In his chest he can feel his heart pounding, then realizes it's hers.

Next to them, outside the van in the rain, a car door slams. An engine starts.

"Nothing terrible is going to happen, Johnnie," Holden says. "I'm going to make sure of that," he's about to pledge before she rises up, stretching her arms around his neck and pulls his mouth to hers. In an instant Holden's ready for her, as if his adult life before this moment has been nothing but a sham and pretense, as if his entire manhood has been one long exercise in waiting for this revelation to occur. He could lose himself in this, he knows— that's the beauty of it. He could lose himself, feel self-lessly *alive*—that's the gift that sex bestows. Baptism through arousal. Orgasm as re-birth. They are linked, now, he and she, like two nucleii pulsing at the membrane of division. She wants him, he can tell she wants him, christ her hand has cupped his balls and she's working all her fingers upward on his dick, when suddenly his brain kicks in. His memory's aroused. "—Johnnie, no, no, wait," he says, "we can't do this. We can't."

He holds her at arm's length.

Her face is radiant with sex, and in his mind he recalls all the women's faces on which he's seen this blush—he recalls this candesence of excitement on the women's faces that his father used to visit in their Sunday "outings" together when Holden was a kid—the way the women used to look, coming from some closed room down the hall or from some room upstairs, women trailing something hidden and exotic on them as his father came to get him where he'd been left to watch TV or read all by himself with a plate of cookies and a glass of Hawaiian Punch in some woman's den or living room. *We'll keep this one secret* his father used to tell him when they got back in the car. *Man-to-man:* your mother doesn't need to know what we've been up to, right, son?

"—why not?" Melanie says, lifting her arms to his neck, giving rise to her breasts.

Holden feels his resolve lessen, his hold on her soften.

Against the roof of the van, the rain, too, changes rhythm, slowing from a persistent percussion to a muted drumming, and through this apparent abatement, outside, he can hear people running toward their cars, a grocery cart accidentally colliding with the rear of the van.

Melanie melts against him again, her hands pressing the back of his neck.

"—please," she says. "Please."

Her lips brush his cheek.

"No one can see us," she says, and the suggestion of secretiveness panics him, the memory of his childhood suspicion of his father's insistence on silence, his father's illicit sex, his adultery, rises like a ghost taking over his body, her words *no one will see us* taking form and fueling his guilt, forming themselves into real shadows behind her, the shapes of Jason, her husband, and her children. *She's married* his conscience tells him: she's newly widowed. She's sick and vulnerable and your old friend's sister. She needs friendship, help, compassion and support, not a quick feel and a fast fuck in a Kmart parking lot.

"—Johnnie, no," he finally has the balls to tell her. "Not this way, not now."

160

He watches her reaction, the way emotions play across her face like shifting weather: cloud of doubt, gust of confusion, no trace of sun; cold front. He sees that source of pain and panic, that occluded darkness, cast its shadow on her person, *be* her person, and he pulls her to him one more time, this time for warmth and comfort, steeling himself, for her sake, against his own desire, because *christ* he wants her, wants her so badly his bones ache. And he senses the redemption that would come, the resultant gift of frenzied intimacy, and he can tell how much she needs its transitive relief, how much she craves it. Again she whispers, "Hold me," and he hugs her to him, wrapping the towel over her shoulders, trying to calm her, soothe her, fulfill all her needs but her most urgent one.

From outside a gusting bout of eddying wind rocks the van on its axis like a cradle, like an ark, tossing them first against one side, then the other, sending groceries sliding against their feet. Then, as they regain their footing in a breath of calm, on the surface of his skin Holden feels an ionized alert, a sudden charge of alternating current that presages a bolt out of the blue, and just as he's about to speak a warning, thunder falls on them with all the rolling force of a glacier slipping off the drop of the planetary horizon, and the light outside the windows flashes as milky green as violent surf when their bones receive the jolt of splitting lightning in their marrow. One, then two, then a successive fusillade of crackling bolts split the air above them until, ever vigilant but never stable, the storm's eye twitches, shifts its aim, moves to seek another unsuspecting target.

"—you okay?" he asks in the ensuing ordinary clamor of the rain.

"—that was *close,*" she breathes.

She looks terrified.

161

He dries her hair, finds a sweatshirt to pull over her, hugs her to him yet again to try to calm her shaking. Almost without thinking he looks at her more closely, then remarks, "You're afraid of rainstorms, aren't you?"

She brightens visibly, as if he'd handed her a piece of something valuable she'd lost.

"How do you know that?" she asks.

"Noah," he answers a bit too slowly to conceal the lie. He smiles at her, as cover.

She tilts her head.

"What else do you know about me?"

Once upon a time, there was a girl who was afraid of rain, Holden finds himself remembering. He looks at her, fine veil of drying curls crowning her with a shimmery corona, and can't answer her at first.

He's thinking of that first page in the first notebook of hers that he'd found—the first page of the first one, chronologically. "Once upon a time," he recites from memory. He dries his hair with a towel, changes into a dry shirt, sneaking looks at her while he starts to stack the groceries and recite to her her own past words: "There was a girl who was afraid of rain." He clears a space for food on the makeshift counter while the rain continues to hammer on the van roof. He peels the lids off tubs of deli food. "She was afraid of rain because of what she'd read in the Book beside her father's bed in her father's bedroom." He hands Melanie a plastic fork.

"Go on," she says.

She's loving this.

"In the Book beside her father's bed in her father's bedroom she'd found a story that told all about her brother. It told about

her brother and a rainstorm. What her brother did in one partic-
ularly spectacular rainstorm. Her brother's name was Noah."

"I remember this," Melanie says, hugging herself. "I really
do—"

Holden lays food out on the counter, clears a space for them
to sit, starts to make a sandwich. The version of this story in the
notebook, the version that he'd read, that he's reciting to her, was
written on the day she'd met Jason, or shortly after—the day
they'd first made love or that she realized she was in love for the
first time in her life—and it was a sweet though falsely epistolary
confession to him, to the object of her new-found devotion. It has
a sweet but faux-naive shared revelation that although she'd had
these childhood fears, the fear of rain, for example, those fears
were childish fears, they were fears that only children have. She
had written in the notebook to explain to her offstage Love that
now that she'd found him, found Jason, now that she'd become a
woman, she'd overcome her fears. She was a child no more. She'd
found Love. Love had initiated her into her womanhood. Love
had conquered all her fear.

"Tell me what you remember," Holden says.

"No, you tell," she says. "You tell first. I want to hear what
Noah told you."

Holden takes a bite of a ham sandwich.

"Tell me stuff about her past," he'd begged Noah on the
phone before this trip, when he'd realized he'd be on the road
with her alone for days.

"Like what?" Noah had answered.

"Stuff. Anything. Innocuous-type stuff. Stuff you don't
remember without help from members of your family. Stuff that
I can talk to her about. What she liked to do. Who she played

with. What she ate for breakfast. Kid stuff. What she was afraid of."

"She was afraid of rain."

"—yeah, she wrote that. She wrote that down, the first line in a journal. That's pretty weird."

"She was weird. Weird kid, wizard weird—maybe brothers always say that about sisters. Always in her head. As for who she played with—I don't remember anybody. No one. She wasn't big on friends. Wasn't big on girlie things. Why do you want to know this?"

"—because she's missing half her life. The rain thing?"

"She was this total tomboy except when it was raining. Always outside, always on her bike or throwing a ball or up a tree or somewhere, except during a rainstorm. Then she turned into a little sissy. Little girl. Scared the pants off her. Because she had this thing about the story in the Bible about Noah."

"What about it?"

"—big deal in her life, first time she read it she came barging into my room when she was like five or six or whenever kids start reading, with the Bible in her hands, madder than hell at me, madder than hell at the whole world."

"Why?"

"Because in the Bible Noah doesn't save her. In the flood. Because the Noah in the Bible doesn't take his sister on the ark. He takes his wife and sons and all their wives and all the animals but she'd read that the Noah in the Bible doesn't take his sister. He leaves his sister there to drown. And that pissed Mel off."

"Does the Noah in the Bible even *have* a sister?"

"—who knows? The thing is, I tried to explain to her that the Noah in the Bible wasn't the Noah in her family, but she wouldn't listen. Every time it rained after that, she'd crawl into a closet,

stay at home. Every night it rained she'd sit at the foot of my bed and stare at me. While I slept. I could feel her watching me. Until the rain stopped. Then she'd give me a sort of look as if to say ha. Gotcha."

When Holden finishes telling her this story, Melanie looks around the van, at their cozy mess, at the rain pouring down the windshield, at the blighted windswept parking lot beyond, and says, "This is a kind of ark we're in, isn't it?"

He touches the back of her hand, makes her look at him and says, "No comparison. This isn't the end of the world."

"I like it when you tell me things," she says.

"I like it when *you* tell me things."

"What else did Noah tell you?"

"That he misses you very much."

"I miss him, too."

"And that he can't wait to see you. Talk to you. Catch up. What's the matter?"

She shakes her head, dismissing it, but Holden presses, until, leaning forward, barely whispering above the rain, she says, "I'm scared to see him."

"Noah? But that's the deal—I'm taking you to him. Why?"

"—scared he might not know me."

"—why?"

"I'm different."

"—different how?"

She touches her face and says, "The way I look."

"—oh, Johnnie . . ."

"I saw this woman back there." She pats her cheeks. "In the mirror. In the supermarket. Me, but not me. Not the me I'm used to. Not the me that's *here.*" She puts her fingers to her forehead. "That's why I like it when you look at me. The way you look at me, the way it makes me feel—like you can tell me who I am. Like you're going to step right up and tell me all about myself. Like if I watch you long enough I'll see myself. Does that make sense?"

"—'watch' me?"

"Read you."

"—'read' me?"

"—you're doing it again. Answering with questions."

"—sorry. Listen. Listen to me. Noah might look different, too, you know. In fact, Noah will look different. Life does that to us. To all of us. It changes us."

"But I'm not sure I'm not dreaming 'Life' most of the time, my 'life,'" she tells him. "Not sure when I'm dreaming or awake. Where I am. When what part of me is real. Except when I'm with you. I don't even know enough about you to feel safe and yet I do. Feel safe. With you."

"What do you need to know about me? I'm an open book, just ask."

She smiles. Digs around in a grocery bag for a Diet Coke and opens it. Takes a sip. Looks at him and says, "Who *are* you?"

"Told you, friend of Noah's. Fellow journalist."

"No, I mean—why do you feel familiar? Why do I feel I know you?"

Holden shakes his head

"Maybe because you need to."

"Why you?"

"You mean, what are my special qualifications for familiarity?"

"I mean why did Noah send you to see me?"

"He didn't send me."

"—who did?"

"—nobody did."

"Then why did you come?"

Holden thinks a moment before saying, "Because rain was forecast."

"I'm serious. Even though I feel safe with you, even though I know we're going to meet Noah, there's this sense of something terrible I told you about. Sense that something terrible is going to happen. To both of us. That it will be my fault. That I could do something—do it now—to stop it all from happening, but I don't know what that is. I don't know what it is that I'm supposed to do. To stop it all from happening."

Their fingertips are touching across the makeshift tabletop.

"Trust, I think," Holden says after a while. "I think the only thing that you're 'supposed' to do is trust me."

The volatile charge between them snaps and simmers again.

"The 'only' thing?" she asks, pointedly.

"And trust Noah. And try not to be afraid of what you don't know. Or what you can't see. Or the rain . . ."

She looks out the window again, at the deluge.

"How long will it take us?"

"—in this?" Holden shrugs. "If we ever get started, three or four days."

She winds her fingers through his.

He raises his soft drink in a toast.

"To the road—to all roads, to wherever they lead."

She joins in the toast.

"To trust," she proposes.

"To Noah," he adds.

Melanie casts her eyes up toward the roof of the van where the rain pounds.

"And to his kind of weather." She smiles.

where they were going

THAT NIGHT HE DREAMS ABOUT ARK ANGELS, ships
built like arks flying through thunderclouds, battling storms on
their feathery wings.

The night's drive had been endless, a monsoon in itself, in
terms of relentless monotony.

They had left the parking lot in a grey pounding rain with five
hours of daylight still left for putting some miles between where
they started from and where they were going.

Holden found himself on a minor route west—way minor—
a miserable choice in this weather, rotten choice in all kinds of
weather, through desolate towns named for no more illustrative
reasons than their primary features—Flat Rock, Gray's Siding,
Guinea Mills, Sprouses Corner.

It had been dark all day, darkened by rainclouds, so dusk came
unnoticed and night, although long overdue, seemed to arrive far
too early.

Holden was exhausted.

Their headlights cut cones through the night, rain catching
strands of light like the traces of bullets.

They had to find some place to stop.

Where that ended up being he would forget as soon as his
head hit the pillow. What he had done with the keys to the van
he wouldn't remember. Nor whether or not he'd undressed himself. If he'd turned off the headlights. Who made the bed. As sleep
overcame him the only thing that he knew in the world was the
drum of the rain on the roof. Eternal drumming. And her touch.
Her touch on his back keeping time with the rain. Maybe it's only
a part of his dream, Melanie's touch on him, writing on his back
through the night. Maybe he dreams it. Dreams he turns into one
of her notebooks. Dreams she asks him again very softly if there

is someone in the world who can help her, who can tell her or show her the truth. Dreams that he tells her I can and gets out the trunk with the notebooks inside. Dreams unlocking the trunk to show her what's inside. Dreams lifting the lid of the trunk to the drumming rain and wings flying up in their faces, hundreds of wings, like a riot of moths in their lust toward a light, their wings shredding to dust like a gust of combustible pixies, a fright of angels, the flight of ark angels from fear into action, from here up to heaven, from guilt into longing. From sorrow to love. From forgetfulness into Eternity.

HE WAKES IN ALARM AT THE QUIET.

Too quiet, he knows.

She's not here.

It's not even warm on her side of the bed and in no time at all he is out of the van, back in again for his shoes.

The van is sitting at the end of a flat grassy field where the terrain falls away down a long languid slope to a stream or a river—maybe a brook—whatever it is he can hear rushing not far away through scrappy wood, elegant birch and tendrils of low-lying fern he can easily run through as soon as he hears something moving down there on the bank by the water.

He calls her name as soon as he sees her—sends the birds flying. She raises her head and smiles at him as though he gets up every morning and just for the fun of it tears through the flora in a mad panic to where she's leaning against the trunk of a willow calmly examining the sole of her foot, naked, wet, clothes she'd been wearing draped over her neck, plastic bag in her hand.

"—hey there," she says. "I came for some pebbles to make a chess set for us and I found this blackberry patch"—she scoops out a handful of red and black berries from the plastic bag—"or rather it found me, I think I picked up a thorn in my—"

He falls on his knees in front of her, his head on her stomach, and sobs.

"—Holden?"

"I didn't know where you were."

"Where could I go without you?"

"—don't ever, ever"—he starts to run his fingers over the scar—"do that again." He runs his tongue on its curve, starts to kiss it, kiss under it, feels the first brush of her pubic hair on his chin, touches it, draws his head back to look at her blond fur as he starts to stroke it, amazed at the inverse effect of her coloration to what he is used to, her skin color darker than her mass of blond hair. He runs his thumb over the plumpness of her mons and as he rubs her she crushes her hand full of berries against her vagina bruising the ripe pulp of them like jam between her thighs. He's never had this taste for women but as if it's as natural as sucking at a mother's breast he gorges himself, exploring with the tip of his tongue for her clitoris through the berries' small seeds. When a sound like a keening rises from her he slips his finger in, surprised at her tightness then he feels her landscape start to quake—when she comes he's shocked by its duration, her muscularity and her strength. He can feel her inner space pumping with pleasure, exciting his own, and when she draws back, her thighs shaking, he doesn't want it to end. She touches his shoulders. Lie down, she instructs. He watches as she slowly lowers herself over him, teasing her nipples in front of his face as she poises herself above his cock then slides her body down until his erection plumbs her breasts, then she squeezes their flesh around him and he's no longer on this planet jesus there's stuff backed up in here waiting for this day to happen since Christmas.

When he comes back down to earth she's in his arms and above them for the first time since the day that they met, the blue sky is unadulterately cloudless.

IT'S LIKE FLYING he realizes.

Like the first time you go up.

You're inside something with manmade wings looking down at clouds through a porthole etched by ice and particles in wind. Far below the manmade quilt of cultivated land in squares of ochre, gold and russet sown in green signals the sacred comfort of a nest abandoned. This is not your element, you think. This is earth from a point of view your evolution never planned for. Beyond the porthole is air that can collapse your lungs and a cold that could turn your blood to ice and crystallize your organs. Released into a freefall from this you'd be dead in half a second, still instead of being gripped by fear you're excited by this set of circumstances. You discover something in you that you never knew was there before: the thrill of losing your control. Oh, you realize. Aren't I brilliant. Aren't I a genius, thirty thousand feet above the earth sipping Diet Coke and popping peanuts down my throat. Not even Leonardo da Vinci got to do this in his lifetime and he was nearer everything Divine in man than I will ever be. Not even Michelangelo on his back beneath the ceiling of the Sistine Chapel got to see this celestial belly, underside of Heaven. *Man!* not even Thomas Jefferson that tarnished cherub—not even Pericles or Archimedes, Isaac Newton, Socrates, Mohammed, Buddha—(maybe Buddha)—men who agonized about the meaning of existence, men who soared on thought but never took their bodies with them on their flights. That's what making love with her was like—like flying—like initiation into an elevated pantheon of geniuses, like rubbing shoulders, shaking hands with giants, men whose imaginations opened doors to states of being that they trusted in but couldn't prove. Augustus Caesar, Marco Polo, Victor Hugo, Darwin, Galileo and Ben Franklin. Navigators of the swell of optimism. Cartographers of hope. And now he's in there with the best of them on top of everything. Making his own weather. Building his own storm anvil, seeing for the first time in his life what it's all about, how the whole thing fits together, feeling the earth *move*.

Making love to her was like being let in on a secret no one else was in on. Like knowing something fabulously simple—obvious—yet mysterious and rare. It was like the time he'd bolted awake on a flight from London to Johannesburg, jolted straight from deep sleep to a deeper panic when he heard the engines cut out. Suddenly both engines had gone dead, the unearthly silence alerting him to imminent disaster. No one else had noticed it. Around him everyone was reading magazines and airplane novels, watching the movie, dozing. Any moment now they would be plummeting to earth, wings torn off like tortured butterflies, and he alone for this split second had been singled out by God to be advance man into Heaven. Everything he thought he'd figure out at some later date, some later moment further down life's happy road—like whether or not he believed there was Life elsewhere in the universe—Big Questions and small—why *doesn't* water run over the lip of a full glass when the ice cubes melt?—all the chances he had pissed away to lead a luminous abundant life suddenly added up to so much more than the meager measure of his accomplishments. Life's final tick was on him and his clock had tocked its last. He was going to die and by some mistake or mir-

acle God had given him and him alone this small reprieve from
full and everlasting ironclad Finality, a nano-mo in which to
finally *get it*, get it right, catch Life's meaning, let those scales fall
from his o so human eyes and discover the right answer to life's
last bonus questions before all hell broke loose. *That's* what making love to her is like. Like the epiphany that would have followed
in the airplane *if* he hadn't swallowed. If he hadn't swallowed in
anticipation of the Act of God to follow. Swallowed and restored
his hearing. Swallowed and turned the plane's engines back on.
Only with this discovery, he thinks, skimming his hand over her
thigh, there's no abracadabra. With this discovery of love there's
no now you see it, now you don't. No open your eyes and voilà
it's no longer there. No blink. No sleight of hand. No swallow.

Is there?

He'd always wondered what it would be like, to feel like this.
To have sex like this. Sex that happened because it had to, sex like
weather. Sex like a planet in upheaval. Explosive, pyrogenic sex.
Sex that peels your skin away. Sex that leaves you skinless.
Mercilessly thrilling sex. Sex that has no self attached. Sacred sex.

—*hey?* she says.

He looks at her.

—you gonna let me in on it?

—in on what? he says.

"In on what's so funny."

He rolls over.

"Me. I am."

She frowns.

He puts his lips against the frownline on her brow.

"—why?" she says.

"Because I'm trying to pretend that there's some way I can
start to tell you how I feel. What all this is like."

"—what this is 'like'?"

"—yeah."

"It's not 'like' something, dodo. I mean there's no approximation. I don't think. If there was they would have marketed it by now. Like the drug in *Brave New World*. Some things just are, you know. Some things exist outside a simile. Without comparison. I mean, you don't ask what Death's a metaphor for, do you."

"—that's why I was laughing. Because if I compare thee to a summer's day it all hangs on where we are in summer."

"—and where are we?"

"When?"

"When we're making love."

"—off the planet. Flying. It's like flying—like hang-gliding. Like what you felt the first time you were in an airplane taking off. That rush, you know. That thrust."

She smiles at him.

"—my goodness."

"—what?"

"Why would you presume I've been in an airplane?"

He blinks.

"—get serious."

"Never been—" She points: "Up there."

"—no hold it. This is, this is just your memory is fucked."

"Well I think if I'd been in an airplane I'd remember it, don't you?" she laughs. "Holden—? What's the matter? What did I say—?"

He takes her hand and spreads it palm down on his chest so she can feel the pounding of his heart.

"—holy christ," she murmurs, "what's the matter with you?"

"I just saw a ghost," he tells her.

She looks up at him.

"—*my* ghost?" she asks.

He nods.

And suddenly the urge is there, in both of them, to fuck their way into a different truth. Only this time it transports them like a whirlwind, makes him feel like he's colliding with the sky.

This time it's like being hit by a tornado.

When he wakes she is staring at him.

How many days has it been since they've left Richmond? One? Two? Nine? Seven?

"You were dreaming," she tells him. "Your eyeballs were racing all around."

"—you dream?"

"Nope. I watched."

"—oh. I never thought of it that way."

"I mean my eyes were open. Watching you. —You make a sucking movement with your mouth. And you grind your teeth."

"Do I come out of this with any of my virility intact?"

"Plus I cut off all your beautiful long hair while you were sleeping."

Up he bolts.

"—just kidding."

He wraps her hair over his fist.

"So did you play with me?" he asks.

"—of course."

He pulls her down and rolls on top.

"—what was it like for you?"

"—like putty in my hands."

He guides himself, without a hand, between her legs and enters her.

And this time it's like skydiving, he thinks. Like falling through a silken golden soft enshrouding cloud.

Or maybe it's like sailing, he explains.

"—jesus, make your mind up. You're either Orville Wright or Christopher Columbus, but all I get to be is navigated."

"—no, no, you're definitely up there, out there, with me."

"—in the crow's nest."

"—in the cockpit."

"You and your nomenclature."

"—You and *yours*," he answers back.

"What's that supposed to mean?" She frowns.

"*Johnnie*," he intones.

She blinks.

"Noah says nobody in your family ever called you Johnnie," Holden tells her.

She stares at him.

"So?" she says.

"So tell me."

"—tell you what?"

"Where 'Johnnie' came from. Who 'Johnnie' is."

She looks blank.

"—okay," he says. "Let's try this. Let's try something different." He shifts his hips on top of hers and starts to trace her eyebrows with his fingertip. "Let's say I want to try to get to know everything about you. How does that sound? Does that sound good?"

She looks noncommittal.

"Why?" she asks.

She lifts her pelvis slightly to excite him, runs her hands over his ass.

"Because," he says seriously, holding her temples between his hands, "I want to know what's in here. Because I want to touch every part of you. I want to get inside. I want to love you in a way that no one ever has. I want to make you feel things about yourself you've never felt before. I want you to remember certain things about your life that you've forgotten so you can know how rare this is. What we have, the love we make. So I can claim my privilege of place."

"—there's no one here but us, Holden," she says. "What do you mean, your 'privilege'?" She watches as he starts to speak, then stops himself. "What kind of 'things'?" she presses.

"Anything," he tells her. "Everything," he lies. "Stuff. Stuff you might not even think could be important." He sees her eyes begin to cloud so he says, "Like this never flying stuff. The way you say you've never been 'up there.' You can't live in this decade, in this century, and not know what being in an airplane's like. There are too many simulations—TV, movies, video games. Everybody knows. Unless you've spent your entire life moving dust around in some remote outpost of Mongolia or the Gobi desert."

She gives a little smile and proposes, "—how 'bout Virginia?"

He props his head up on an elbow.

"Let's get this straight. You expect me to believe you've lived your entire life in Virginia. Even worse: *you* believe you've spent your whole life here."

"What is 'even worse' supposed to mean? What's so terrible about staying in the same place all your life?"

"—unadventurous, for starters. Given that what will probably go down in history as the most distinguishing aspect of this century in history will be migrations, movements of populations either as refugees, because they need to fill their bellies . . ."

He senses she's about to start to disagree with him so he quickly changes tack and argues, "But that's not what I was talking about when I said 'even worse.' I was talking about whether or not you lived in one place all your life. Maybe you have. I've no way of knowing. I don't have that information. You do. In here." He taps her head. "That's what I was talking about. What you believe in yourself."

"—what I 'believe'?"

"What you remember. What you don't remember."

He averts his eyes and casts his gaze along her body.

"Like what?" she says.

Not consciously aware of what he's doing he lets his hand fall across the scar from her Cesarean.

"—*things*," he says.

He lifts his hand off her belly when he realizes what he's touching, as if it's something that might scorch him.

"—things," he says more calmly, "like love."

She looks at him as if she's never heard the syllable before, and she repeats the word.

". . . *'love.'* "

The way she says it makes the word sound hollow, and he feels a cramp inside his heart.

"People you've—" he starts to say. "Men you've loved before me."

She stares at him.

"—how you learned to make love the way you do. How you learned to use your body like you do."

"—that's what you think? I 'use' my body?"

"You can't believe I'm the first man you've made love to," he says tenderly, but then regrets it. "You're too experienced," he adds hearing—too late—what a mess of it he's making. "I mean—"

He casts around for some way to get out of this. "You know what you're doing, right? You're experienced. Right? So where do you think you learned all that?"

"—'learned' it?"

Because he's never seen her look like this before he doesn't read it right, at the beginning—her expression. He clocks her gathering confusion, but he doesn't see the hurt that he's inflicting. How did he get into this? All he had intended was to point out to her that she was too sophisticated, too worldly wise to support the point of view that she trafficked all her life within a radius of several hundred Old Dominion miles, but when he'd had to cough up concrete evidence to prove his case, instead of mentioning her wisdom, grace and glancing wit the first words from his mouth said less of her stunning attributes than of his own sickmaking insecurity. It was obvious to him where she'd learned her way around a cock, learned how to tease and hold him in her hand, learned how to run her tongue along the primary vein from his scrotum to his head, learned how to take a penis in her mouth without hesitation, how to keep her teeth behind the cushion of her lips, how to move her hips when she was on him in that way the French call *la diligence de Lyon* in honor of the stagecoach of the same name which used to rock its passengers like babies in a cradle twisting with a slight kick from the left to right then twisting back again while at the gallop, diligently headstrong, from Paris to Lyons, making certain everybody came on schedule—no one moved like that without a lot of practice. No woman he had ever known had ever moved like that *at all*. It was obvious to him that she'd learned these flourishes, these knowledgeable gestures, these tricks of the trade, from years and years of undiminished soul-enriching brain-blasting sex with her dead husband and that he, Holden, was the Inheritor of that experience, not its Creator.

He, Holden, was only number two in line, standing in the other's shadow.

"—things you do," he's trying to explain.

"—what 'things'?"

"—you know."

He doesn't see her desperation.

"—people don't just stand up from all fours," he says, "and give automatic great sex the way you do without a long privately tutored learning process, you know."

Her eyes grow large with tears.

Her lip begins to tremble.

"I never did," she starts to say. The sentence catches in her throat. "—all I do is follow you—it seems so natural—everything we do just happens," she protests. "Everything we do is brand new for me—how can you think otherwise? Everything we do I've never done before—I'm learning everything from you—"

Her shoulders heave.

She hides her face behind her hands.

"—aw, Johnnie geez," he says.

He pries her fingers from her eyes and starts to cover them with kisses.

"—I'm sorry," he tells her. "—hey. Don't cry, Johnnie. Listen. Look at me. I've never felt this way before. You understand? Forgive me. Johnnie, please. Come on. That'a girl. Kiss me. I'm just trying to explain how much I love you . . ."

And maybe it *was* true. Maybe she hadn't ever loved like this before.

Come to think of it—it must be true. It had to be. Intimate communion, in his view, intimate communion of this nature can't

180

strike twice in a single lifetime. And even if it wasn't true, it looked like she believed it was. Even if it wasn't true it appeared she had no memory, she could not recall the other one, so that there was a way that he could make himself believe that it was true, too, by pretending that she had no past, that hers was a life that only really started when she met him.

That's what all lovers do, anyway, isn't it? Deceive themselves? Forget the past and start all over again?

Every time they made love it was more beautiful than the time before—more profoundly scary—so perhaps he *was* the Adam in the Paradise, not the snake, not the usurper. After all, what memories did God give Adam at Creation? How many memories did Eve have when she first awoke in Eden?

Fewer than Adam had, at that moment, that's for sure.

So if other people Start All Over, wipe the slate of memory clean and wake up fully formed adults halfway through lives in Eden, why couldn't he and Melanie? What was so morally unsavory about that? If it was so ethically questionable to give your past the ol' heave-ho why were so many people doing it? Start your own two-column list with one column comprising all the Stand By Me songs you can remember and the other column all the Just Walk Away ones running through your head and guess which column will be longer? Lord, here they were deep in country music territory just a jugtoss from the border with Kentucky and if he could claim a greenback every time a Time Heals Every Wound tune played on the radio he'd have himself a handy fortune.

If he could keep her from remembering for just a little while—well not "keep" her from it, there was no way that he could do that—if he could keep her in the present without the past intruding, then they might have a chance to forge a union made from love strong enough to stand up to that past history. Or so he thinks, sometimes, while he's lying still beside her in those first nights in the milky light of a full moon in the blue hills falling from the granite hogback ridges that link the Appalachian chain. A desperate plan, he knows, and one that's got zero going for it save a sort of cosmic lust, a larger than life sex urge—which is no small force, let's face it, in the ranks of history's causal battalions.

Still, central to his sexual desire for her is something joined to sex but intrinsically asexual—difficult to describe in any words other than religious ones. But even religious words—"sacred," "holy," "pure"—inadequately describe what he refers to in his nightly conversations with himself as The Look. Unlike other women he's been with Melanie keeps her eyes on him when they make love. It's not a casual gaze, a dreamer's gaze, or a spectator's: it's a seeker's. What it seeks, he believes, is something only he could give her. It's a pointed Look, clear and sharp as a syringe, bright as needles, and addictive. Addictive because although it is a searching gaze, like a beacon, at its center is a focal field of light, a reflector like a lighthouse mirror and what he sees when he beholds the Look are the dimensions of a soul cut loose from physical restraint—maybe his soul, maybe hers, maybe the soul of human love—unattainable perfection, a profound stillness, inner peace, an infinite tableau onto which he can project any thing and all things: a soul before its birth: a soul unscored by death and time: a Stanley Kubrick cine-vision of a soul suspended somewhere between earth and heaven.

In her eyes while they are making love he sees a thing he's never seen before, something fundamentally thrilling, the Look of something that exists beyond Time—the Look of innocence. Of the eternal. Emptiness. Of everything and nothing.

Purity.

Forgetfulness.

Oblivion.

That's what its pulling power is for him—when he stares into her eyes while they're making love her Look induces forgetfulness in him, like the legendary drug nepenthe in Greek mythology, it takes him to a state of mind where he forgets himself, surrenders his entire being to the transport of their sex only to re-enter a conscious state—re-enter his body, so to speak, reintegrate himself like the materializing special effect after climax.

Slowly, in the moments after sex, he comes back into his sense of self, into his personality, his history, his set of facts, his fingers and his toes.

He comes back.

She doesn't.

At first he doesn't notice. In those first few days of heady sex, of nearly round-the-clock fucking, he doesn't see that she is *always* in that distant state of mind, that the Look—so magnetic while they're making love—is *always* there, *always* in her eyes.

What seems "eternal," "timeless," "pure" about the Look while they're making love seems merely blank and empty when they aren't.

Outside sexual context, without the physical connection of their sex, when she looks at him her gaze is dis-embodied, eerily remote, as though she depends on their communion, slakes her thirst with intercourse to supply her an illusory existence.

An intact history.

One that she is making up as she goes along.

One that she is making up while they're making love.

He doesn't see it at the start, how could he? He can barely string two coherent thoughts together in his passion—he can barely speak.

It's only when he starts to talk of love that he first notices.

Only when he speaks the words *I love you* for the first time does he see the emptiness that's really there, the Nothing that stands in for something when the mind forgets, the Vacancy of meaning in a life whose history's been erased.

He starts to really see it on the night the moon is full.

They'd been on the road four nights—though Time, as an accountant for love's balance sheet, is full of tricks.

They stayed two nights in the same field then broke camp abruptly before dawn the third day when the van was surrounded by a herd of lowing cattle. Holden drove the van out of the field to a paved road in his underwear and aimed them west toward the Blue Ridge Parkway but pulled off the road again after an hour to make love beside an unnamed creek overexcited with small ecstatic rapids.

On the third day they hit Interstate 81 at Roanoke and got on it thinking maybe they would take a short run northeast between these ridges to the Natural Bridge, but they left the fast road at the nearest interchange and circled back toward Cumberland Gap on the slower Route 11, acknowledging by doing so that a six-lane highway, even an American one, is no place for coupling.

Backroads, with their episodes in history, their hand-painted weathered signs begging and exclaiming hope and fortune, commerce and belief, livebait and Jesus, catfish and The Lord, seemed more their style, more like what they needed. Abandoned barns. Deserted houses with storm cellars. Roads that told you there's no reason to be hurried. Slow-banked lanes of black macadam swerving to a scenic lookout point where the summer sunset paints lofty crimson ranges over these cool ridges dressed in misty veils of radiation blues. For the lovestruck, few itineraries can be found in the whole country more scenic, more melancholy, more edenic than the route west-southwest on the Skyline Drive, America's most graceful road, down into my ol' Kentucky home.

The towns grow smaller, like Petri dishes preserving microcultures—sleepy foothill towns with names like Hurt, Lone Gum, Scruggs, Retreat. Not so long ago this part of the country, where the first hogback ridges transect the continent from right to left, used to be the Great Frontier—it used to be The West. Pillaged from the Cherokees, these counties, plus the area across the mountains, became the province of the burly boys, illiterate roughnecks like Daniel Boone conversant in half a dozen tribal languages or blasted to a boneheaded moronic recidivism from imbibing too much moonshine like the Hatfields and McCoys.

People out here don't much like big government and may not even much like people on the other ridge or in the valley or on the other side of this here fence. But when it comes to making music or making bourbon, God sure blessed them with the country for it and threw in some extra backbone, extra spine, called the Appalachian Chain, the Allegheny, Blue Ridge, Shenandoah and the Cumberland. Weren't the Rockies, hell no, nor even the Sierras, but those further western ranges didn't ever give rise to any bluegrass music, neither. Loretta Lynn was no *uranium* miner's daughter was she, no. There is no escaping bluegrass blended with Jesus on the local radio, and in the evenings, even while he's sleeping Holden keeps it tuned in way down low so the meanings of the words are lost but the rhythms of the heartbreak of the music and the preachers' exhortations to *love jesus!* underscore their love making.

On the fourth night, the night of the full moon, they'd descended from Pinnacle Peak onto the Wilderness Road and are camped at a site beneath a stand of hickory and gum trees going

185

prematurely gold in the summer drought beside a clearing on a dirt road between Pineville and Corbin in Kentucky.

And whether it's because of the full moon or because he's depleted all his energy reserves making nonstop love for the past four days, Holden is as hungry as a bear.

Holden could eat like there's no tomorrow, so for the first time since they've been on the road they actually camp out—they gather wood and clear the ground and build a fire and they cook.

Or rather, Holden goes along with Melanie as she tells him what wood to gather, does what Melanie tells him to do to clear the ground, and Holden watches Melanie build the fire and prepare their meal.

"—you've done this before," he notes like he's some detective.

He watches her turn a hickory spit of ribs over the flames and thinks, Right again, Holmes. She was the mother of four sons. She knows her way around a campfire.

He stares at the moon. "Let's stay out here tonight," he says. "What d'you say?"

After they've eaten and the fire's dying down and the critters start to fill the nighttime airwaves with their critters' nighttime news, and he and she are hunkered down together on backbreaking ground inside their down-filled nest staring at the diamond stars, an elaborate tiara crowning the moon behind her snow-white bridal veil, Holden holds her in his arms and tells her, "Once upon a time, according to a Cherokee legend, everything lived in the sky."

She shifts so she can see more sky and says, "I like this story."

"When the sky got too full of spirits," he tells her, "a dung beetle came down on a thread and lowered herself into the widest river and came up with a ball of mud from the river bottom. But

186

the ball of mud was too slippery for any creature to live upon so a great bald eagle flew down to dry it with the flapping of its wings. It flapped and flapped until the ball of mud was almost dry but all its efforts soon exhausted it and it died from its exertion and fell into the ball of mud. And where it fell to its death with its wings still outstretched became the Appalachian Mountains." He points to the outline on the horizon and says, "Over there."

She lifts her head a little from his shoulder so she can see where he is pointing.

"Padge taught me that," he says. "It's not my favorite Creation Myth but I never really appreciated it until I saw these mountains. I think Padge liked it because its heroes—the beetle and the eagle—fall out of the sky. Like Padge. Padge used to step out of the cargo bay of airplanes into clouds as casually as someone stepping off their porch to pick up their morning paper."

"You talk about him a lot," she says.

He turns his head toward her and senses the complex perfume of the fire in her hair. It's true that, although they haven't talked as much as he imagines most new lovers do, filling in the canvas of their lives-as-lived before they met each other, sketching flattering likenesses of their former selves, when they do talk it's Holden who talks most, attempting always to solicit joint exchange of information with her, always encountering a blank.

He'd talked to her about his boyhood, about the things that he remembered from his past, and inevitably all those things included Padge. There seemed no way of talking about himself, about the scenery, about science and the world he lived in, about the weather, about anything, without talking about Padge because his grandfather had been one of those figures who radiated life and made things happen like a force of nature.

if

"—how could you not talk about a person who not only taught you to ride a bicycle but also showed you how to make snow flurries in the kitchen freezer?" Holden says.

"But you make it sound like he taught you everything," she says.

"—well, he did," he says, easing her nipple to erection between his finger and his thumb under the sleeping bag. "—*almost.*" He starts to kiss her but before he can she says, "What do you think he would be doing if he was still alive today?"

The question seems so weirdly casual Holden rolls over so he can look at her.

"—what makes you ask a thing like that?"

"Nothing in particular," she shrugs.

He fingers a strand of her hair and sees the embers of the fire reflected like a sunset in her eyes.

"I don't know," he says, reluctant to bring the dead-as-Dead into their conversation. Into the night. It was one thing to talk about Padge as a living memory, quite another to talk about him as no longer being there, counted with the living. "I don't know," he repeats. "I never think of him as being . . ." His voice trails off. "I don't think of him that way," he finally says. "He had such enthusiasm, you know, for everything—well, for weather, really. He was such a weather freak. Storms . . ." He slides back down beside her so he can stare back at the sky. "He was obsessed with extreme meteorological phenomena—t-storms, thunder, lightning, cyclones . . . tornadoes." He turns his head to check her profile. *Don't mention the war,* he thinks. That famous joke. Don't talk about the war to any Germans. Don't mention it. Pretend it's not a sore spot, that it didn't happen. Turn a blind eye, be polite. Imagine how much peace of mind might fall on both attacker and attackee if they could forget. Just imagine. So *don't mention the*

188

tornado part of him is saying as he stares at her, at her immovable features, her mask of serenity empty of expression, the only flicker of movement in it arising from the lick of flame reflected in her eyes. And suddenly something kicks in him, the spirit of rebellion, maybe, or his conscience, the stalking ghost of all his journalistic training.

"—yeah, tornadoes," he repeats, watching her for any trace of a reaction, finding none. Should he pursue this? He feels his heartbeat hasten. "I imagine," he says slowly, his eyes still focused on her, "he'd still be doing what he always did—going after explanations, searching for the answers. Chasing storms. I mean—I have to think he'd be the same, you know? Same Padge he always was. It wasn't like he lived centuries ago and spent his life engaged in what is now a dead pursuit . . . like, I don't know, like alchemy. Like diagnosing anthrax. His pursuit was weather. How weather works. What makes it happen. And that hasn't changed, the weather hasn't. Global warming, yeah—but severe storms are severe storms, always have been, always will be, their particulars don't change much over time. Only the technology changes, our skills for forecasting. Instead of wizards and men of magic, now we have satellites and men of science. Padge was always one part hocus-pocus, three parts science. So I have to guess he'd be the same today. But instead of chasing clouds in a surplus Army air corps plane he'd be one of those guys you see on TV with those high-tech vans with split-screen radar/sonar digital positioning and mobile phones. Running down the eye of a tornado."

He holds his breath.

She doesn't move.

Her family died in a tornado and she doesn't even blink, and he allows the silence to accumulate between them like a surface film, like a membrane. Or like a wall. And suddenly he intuits emptiness, feels its presence like the chill reach of darkness at the entrance of a vast uncharted cave.

Sadness falls on him, unbeckoned sadness, sadness that unbeckoned memories can sometimes bring, and he hears himself telling her, "Padge died on a night like this, a night with a full moon."

He hears the way his own voice—willful, strident—softens as his memory speaks.

"I was still at Harvard, in my third year, Pooh and Kanga had been down in Washington by then for several years. And late one night the campus police came to my room and said they had some old guy downstairs they've picked up wandering around the Yard in his pajamas who's given them my name and sure enough when I go with them there's Padge in his striped pajamas and terry-cloth robe and leather slippers with his hair standing out all around his head like he's been electrocuted."

Holden stops and listens to the night as if trying to make out what these noises have to do with the scene he sees so vividly before him in his memory.

"—he looked like, he looked like he'd passed through some kind of super-ionized force field, or he'd just been struck by lightning. He was acting dizzy and disoriented, he couldn't quite connect to where he was and god knows how he got there but he lit up like a Christmas tree as soon as he saw me so the police were glad to let him go. And the thing is—the thing is—he had always been a little mad, you know? So I didn't, I didn't see the signs. I didn't know enough, I guess, to look for them."

He hears the voice of his own memory quaver with emotion.

"I mean, even doctors tell you they can't always read the outward signs of stroke. Unless there's something, you know, major like paralysis or speech impairment. He just kinda didn't seem to know how he had gotten there but Padge was always like that, distracted in reality, free-trading with those inner voices, so I put him in my car and started to drive him back to his house instead of doing what I should have done which was take him to a doctor right away. Take him to Mass General. But I didn't . . ."

Holden feels the weight of sadness on his chest and when he takes a breath he hears it shiver.

". . . and he seemed okay in the car—quiet, though. Quieter than usual, but I was acting pretty pissed off about having to get up in the middle of the night to drive him home so I didn't think too much about why he was so quiet. And then suddenly he leans forward and points through the windshield to the full moon in the sky straight in front of us and says, 'Moon,' like he's just identified the word. Then he sits back and says, 'You know something, Holden? I always wanted to go there.' And that's the last thing he ever said."

From somewhere in his memory the moment that he pulled into his grandfather's driveway and switched the engine off and turned to Padge and raised his hand to touch him and began to realize he was dead—those moments, that one awful moment, all come flooding back on him and he's no longer just a newly minted lover in her arms he's a person with a complement of living ghosts, a presence with a past, a man who can both rejoice in love and mourn.

As he weeps, she cradles him. She rocks him in her arms and whispers, "—there, there. —there, there, Holden."

And when the full force of his memory has ebbed, its shadow cleansed by tears, and he looks at her again, he sees fully for the first time the face of one who hasn't seen, like someone exiled to the darkside of the moon, the ultimate transcendence of the incandescent side of grief.

on the line

HEADING WEST the voice is saying AND LOSING ITS
IDENTITY.

"... let's repeat that for the benefit of all you folks north of
Cumberland between Hazard and the Middle Fork—that storm
we saw buildin out there earlier this mornin is now *headin west and
losin its identity*—it's official, we have it from the big boys—so y'all
go on ahead an' hang that wash out on the line 'cause we're plain
in this heat with no relief in sight. An' that's it this weather hour on
your Kentucky Storm Watch station K-Thirteen Ninety-nine."

"—shame," Melanie remarks. She tilts her sunglasses up
and wipes the mist of perspiration from the bridge of her nose.
"—these fields sure could stand some water . . ."

"—this stuff?" Holden asks. "What is this stuff?"

She halfway smiles.

"—well that 'stuff' "—she points to a field of broad brown-
leafed plants streaming past the window on his side of the van—
"is what we call tobacco. And this"—she points to yellow stuff on
her side of the road—"is that little Old World something we call
sorghum."

"—oh, sorghum. —yeah. You hear a lot about that in your
agricultural briefings. So that's sorghum, well I'll be. What the
fuck do we use sorghum for?"

"Syrup, silage. Pig food. It shouldn't be this color, actually . . ."

"What color should it be?"

"—greeny blue."

"—christ it's hot, should we turn the air conditioning on?"

"—no I like the windows down."

"—let's hope we find a gas pump between here and Corbin . . ."

"—there'll be one in Barbourville," she says like she knows
what she's talking about and Holden glances over at her and
blows her a kiss. She's wearing a plain white sleeveless shirtdress

192

and a pair of Keds they bought at a Kmart outside Roanoke. She's tied her hair in a ponytail with a rubber band high up on her head and she looks like one of those high-school girls you see in fifties movies.

"You look pretty, Johnnie," Holden tells her.

She vamps at him over the sunglasses. "Well, it's not every day a girl's invited to a real Kentucky Colonel's . . ."

As usual this morning he had woken to her gone—something he'd gotten used to when he woke each morning, but this morning was different because they'd spent the night outside. If he woke in the middle of the night she was always there, by his side, wide awake, watching him. But if he woke as the day was breaking she was always gone. He would lie and listen to the birds, sometimes fall asleep again, and she'd be back after a minute, maybe two. Or so it seemed. Not until this morning did he realize that he'd never seen her sleeping. Not until this morning had he ever stirred from sleep to watch her leave. Maybe it was because he hadn't woken in the night, as usual, to make love again—after he'd relived his feelings from the night that Padge had died he'd fallen into deep unbroken sleep until he felt her turning in the sleeping bag then felt a chill along his body where she'd been, felt the hard cold ground beneath his bones, and woke. Only because his throat was still constricted from crying himself to sleep the night before was he not able to voice her name as he pushed his shoulders off the ground and opened his eyes.

She was standing about twenty feet away from him, stark naked—searching. Looking around for something. Searching the ground. Walking back and forth.

. . . and writing.

—*shit*, he thought.

He stood up, suddenly alert, and pulled the sleeping bag around him. He hadn't seen this writing shit since the day that they left Richmond.

It looked really nuts this time, robotic gestures like a record needle jumping in a vinyl groove, like her arm was ricocheting off competing motions.

She looked like she was going crazy.

"—Johnnie?"

When he reached for her she spun her back to him and like a flapping eagle with the bag around him Holden leaped in front of her.

"—hey. —my girl," he urged, his voice nearly a whisper.

She stared at him but didn't register him at all.

He backed away, cold all over.

"—*can't find it,*" she breathed.

Cold around his ankles, like a shackle.

Cold like killing steel inside his thighs.

She stood stock-still except for a shiver in her spine and closed her eyes.

When she opened them again she looked at him with recognition and tears streamed down her cheeks.

"—something's lost," she told him softly.

"—I know."

"—I have to find it."

"—I know you do."

He wrapped himself around her, seeking warmth.

"—you'll find it," he promised, "I'll help you. We'll find it together."

They stood like that, cocooned, for a brief moment, peaty musk of the cold fire from the night before expanding with the first rays of the sun, and within a minute she had brought him where she always did on waking every morning, hard and storming to her warmth.

Kentucky fried.

Now that they are off the cool blue ridges down on the alluvial plain, heat takes its tenancy like something elementally rank and criminal taking to the mattresses: sits all day and doesn't move except in sudden gusts of hot explosive wind like showers of stinging bullets, hail of gunfire across the skin.

In Barbourville the signs counting down the distance to Colonel Harland Sanders Cafe and Museum in Corbin are already five a mile.

And that's exactly where they're headed, soon as they gas up.

The sun is just about the highest it will get all day and as Holden stands at the service island in the heat next to the tanks, the rising fumes shimmy cobra dances off the metal of the van.

Across the road the random gusting plows a narrow aisle through whatever that brown stuff is growing over there, but none of it is crossing to refresh this side of the road.

When he's filled both tanks, before he pays, he sticks his head through the open window on the driver's side and says, "You want anythin from in thar, Daisy Mae? A Dr Pepper?" and as she smiles at him and shakes her head and he starts to move away he feels a hot wall of air like the exhaust from a blast furnace hit the backs of his legs and he watches it gust through the van like one of those leaf-blowers, going straight through the window on his side and out the window on hers, rifling through the loose debris on the dashboard and picking up a piece of paper, sending it sailing dizzily out over the road like a classroom glider.

Next thing he knows he hears the blare of an airhorn, like a signal from a ship at sea, from a hauler tearing down the road as Melanie hurls herself out of the van and sprints across the road in front of it and disappears at speed into the field of chest-high brown stuff on the other side.

A bright green John Deere tractor with its plow in tow belching diesel fumes has to swerve a little to miss Holden as he races after her, crashing through the brown stuff over moguls of crusty earth, ten hundred million shitty little black things seemingly too small to harbor organized biology suddenly fill the air from lairs on the undersides of dusty drooping leaves. She's fast, but he is faster, and this time he grabs her with no second thoughts of tenderness.

"—what the hell is going on?"

"—that's it—that's it! —it went out the window!"

He clenches his fist around her wrist, sweat pumping through every pore of his body, his pulse doing tom-tom rhythms on his temples while he stands in the buzzing and the fusty heat and studies her, trying like mad to catch his breath.

He waits until he's calm and then he says, "We're in trouble here, you know that?"

Her eyes are gleaming.

For the first time this week her eyes have come alive.

"What are you up to, Johnnie?"

"—you're hurting me, Holden."

He lifts her arm, then hurls it back at her as if he's tossing down a gauntlet. He kneels down to cool off.

His skin is hurting him.

He lowers his head between his knees and joins his palms behind his neck.

Minutes go by while she searches. He hears her messing through dry crumbling leaves. The whole fucking field smells like

196

a cigar factory. Tobacco. "—*shit,*" he breathes. A bristly insect with divining rods for legs and pus-filled knobs for eyes alights upon his arm. "—fuck *this,*" he swears and kills it. He goes to find her.

And is surprised to meet her only yards away, standing with her arms wrapped around her torso, rocking, looking at the sky.

When she sees him she raises her right arm in an arc and says, "—it flew out."

"—Johnnie . . ."

He needs to tell her they can't go on this way.

"—it flew out the window!"

He shoves his hands down in his pockets.

"—big deal," he tells her.

"—just like that," she says and gestures to explain. "—off the dashboard."

"—off the dashboard," he repeats, hearing the raw frustration in his voice.

"—I had to get it!"

"Oh well that's all right, then. You had to get it. You had to fucking almost get us killed to get it."

"—yes!"

"—and did you get it? Did you Johnnie? Where is it? Do you have the goddamn gas receipt or whatever the fuck it was that flew off the dashboard that you had to get? Do you? Show it to me— I'm dying to see it. I'm dying to see what could be so important about some fucking thing we've left on the fucking dashboard of the fucking car—or any fucking thing for that matter that anyone could fucking leave on a dashboard of a fucking car—"

And that's it, that's how truth arrives, a knockout punch, shock to the ol' system, shattered solar plexus, an astonishment, the dazzling light, a sizzling blinding insight. Something that was on the dashboard flew out of the car—something dear to her, something precious, flew out in the wind that came before the storm—and she had to get it—*so she got out of the car.*

This woman did.

This woman that he loves.

On a road beside a field like this one.

She, alone.

Before the tornado.

And he sweeps her up, crushing flesh and bones, binding her to him in his guilt, his passion and his sorrow until through the cage her ribs make he can feel his lonesome heart combine with hers.

WELCOME TO CORBIN, KENTUCKY! HOME OF COLONEL HARLAND SANDERS' FAMOUS SECRET BLEND!

Or if you missed that:

WELCOME TO CORBIN, KENTUCKY! HOME OF AMERICA'S FAST-FOOD PIONEER!

HOME OF THE SUNDAY DINNER SEVEN DAYS A WEEK!

HOME OF THE ORIGINAL RECIPE!

"For years," the automated Voice in the Harland Sanders Museum next door to the Harland Sanders Cafe tells you, "the Colonel carried the secret formula for his Kentucky Fried Chicken in his head and the spice mixture in his car."

"—well that's a relief," Holden observes.

"In 1935 Governor Ruby Laffoon"—yes, Ruby Laffoon—"of Kentucky made Harland an official Colonel of the Commonwealth for his contributions to the State's culinary achievement," the Voice elaborates, "and by 1976 an independent survey ranked the Colonel as the world's second most recognizable celebrity."

Melanie and Holden lock eyes and mutually ponder who was first most.

Elvis, they spontaneously decide.

Unless it was Mickey, he says.

Or Santa, she offers. Or Christ.

"Is Christ a celebrity?"

"—well he's on the radio."

"—but not on Oprah—*yet* . . ."

Although the dining room of the Colonel's original café would be cooler, they opt for a table under the ceiling fans on the porch next to the lawn where kids are playing. Iced tea arrives without being asked for, along with the biscuits. Despite the heat Holden orders The Classic—six pieces of chicken, cole slaw, gravy, mashed potatoes—because after the drama of this morning, he's feeling better, he's feeling good, because he's in love.

"We're going to be okay, you know," he tells her, taking her hands in his across the table. "I love these hands," he says, kneading her fingers with his, feeling the strength in them, accomplished hands molded by chores, used to the daily routines of a life.

Her face is scrubbed clean of the dust and the sweat from the tobacco field and she's changed her tobacco-stained dress for one of his T-shirts and a cotton skirt. Her hair is plaited in one braid falling down her right shoulder and she's wearing a straw hat. Holden longs to tell her what's in his heart, what he is feeling, but their food arrives and, anyway, he thinks, there's time for all that. There's plenty of time.

"—hey, 'Chicken Facts,'" he reads off his paper placemat. "'Laid head to claw'—there's a concept—'KFC chickens consumed worldwide would stretch 284,000 miles.'" He tucks into his own, still reading. "'They would circle the Earth at the Equator 11 times or stretch from the Earth approximately 59,000 miles past the moon . . .'"

He stops to contemplate that particular vision. Hens in space. Star Peck.

"'... today the Colonel's Original Recipe of 11 herbs and spices first served here in Corbin is locked away in a safe in Louisville. Only a handful of people know the multimillion-dollar recipe and they are under contract to safeguard its confidentiality ...'"

He watches her lick some confidentially seasoned *jus* from her fingers and feels, yet again, how fucking easily he's turned on by her.

"Life is funny isn't it?" she says.

He's so turned on he can't answer.

"I mean such a fuss about a recipe. How many ingredients do they claim it's got?"

She does the finger licking again.

"—eleven," he mutters.

She does it again.

"—well," she muses.

Again.

"—I'd wager six. I think they're exaggerating."

"I want to make love to you, Johnnie," Holden confesses just as their waitress arrives to clear the plates. "—an' here I was goin to offer y'all some dessert," she camps. When she brings their apple pies and coffees Holden says she's the first Kentuckian he's ever met. "—aside from the guy at the gas station this morning. I mean don't get me wrong, I've met maybe a hundred thousand people in my lifetime in countries all over the world, but you just don't meet that many from Kentucky, you know what I mean?" and along with the check she slaps a pamphlet down on the table that's titled "Famous Kentuckians."

"—something I said?" he asks Melanie, reaching for his wallet. "—here's one, 'John Colgan'—ever heard of him? 'Developed chewing gum in 1879.' 'John T. Thompson,'" he reads, counting out money, "'Inventor of the Tommygun.'—oh, and hey . . . Johnny Depp's from Kentucky!" He clocks her blank look. "Johnny Depp?" he tries again. "—okay, so we've never heard of Johnny Depp . . . Hunter Thompson?" A blank. "—here's one for you, *Louis Brandeis.*" She brightens. "—thought you'd recognize that one. —geez, there's loads of people from Kentucky here, Diane Sawyer, D. W. Griffith . . . the Everly Brothers . . . the Judds . . . W. C. Handy . . . Victor Mature, wow-wee . . . Harry Dean Stanton . . . Gus Van Sant . . . and, hey, *both* Abraham Lincoln *and* Jefferson Davis . . . jesus, both of them. Born less than thirty miles from one another . . . can you believe that? —Johnnie?" Her attention is focused on the table next to them and as she stares toward it she absentmindedly strokes the empty place on her ring finger where her wedding band should be on her left hand.

Holden follows her gaze to a man holding a newspaper in front of him at the table to his right and the page that's facing out that Melanie is staring at is that page where they run photographs of engaged couples and newlyweds and Holden almost can't believe his eyes.

"—um, excuse me," he says to the man behind the paper. "—yeah. —sorry. —is that today's *Washington Post?* Can I ask you where you got it? I mean, if there's a place to buy one here in Corbin . . ."

"Have mine," the man says, folding it up.

"—oh no I couldn't . . ."

"—sure you could, I was just checkin what I'm missin on TV while I'm on the road," he says, standing up and putting on a crisp white Panama hat. He touches its brim and bows to Melanie and places the paper Wedding Announcements page up on the table between them.

And there's Sydney.

And Sydney.

And Sydney's C-cups.

"—*jesus,*" Holden mutters. What a botched job, he thinks. Kanga was right. They look like two bowling balls on a shelf.

He spreads the paper between them.

"—this is my best friend from college, Sydney, and . . . Sydney," he enthuses to Melanie, not really seeing how far she's retreated into herself. "—geez, look at the two of them," Holden marvels. Posing like that. For their engagement. That's so not like the old Sydney—what's happened to him, they look like two yuppies, Holden thinks. Two Young Republicans. What would they think of his current situation—unemployed, on the road with this woman—what would they think if they could see him, what would they say to him now?

"I should call them," he says. "I gotta call them. Sydney asked me to be his best man and I let him down, I just up and left . . ." He looks around for a pay phone and spots one at the far end of the porch. "—will you be okay here by yourself for a minute? Huh?" He looks at her. "—Johnnie?" She nods. "—okay I'm gonna go make a call. I'll be right over there. Okay? Look at me." He doesn't read what's going on with her at all. "—be right back," he says, touching her cheek as he goes.

It's one of those pay phones with no acoustics where you have to plug up one ear so you can hear with the other. He gets Information for the District of Columbia but has to stand close to the wall and turn his back to the lawn so the operator can hear him when he says Sydney's name because kids are shouting behind him in the play yard out there where there are swings and a sandbox and a merry-go-round and a jungle gym inside a giant plastic chicken. He turns toward Melanie and sees her sitting at the table, back-lit in profile, watching the children at play, and he's touched by how calm she looks, how serene and how lovely. And he thinks how lucky he is. He thinks how lonely her life would be without him—how graceless his would be without her—and on sudden impulse, feeling expansive, flushed with his own good fortune, feeling forgiveful, after the operator recites Sydney's number, he says, "—and in Georgetown. Mr. Peter Garfield, please."

He is vaguely aware of Melanie's movement while he's dialing his father's telephone number but he's mostly aware of how much his hand's shaking, how spongy he feels in his legs like the way he used to feel when he first started interviewing heads of state.

A woman answers.

Holden takes a breath and prays his voice will come out steady. "—um, may I speak to Mr. Garfield, please?" he asks.

He thinks his voice sounds that wavy way a person's voice does when they're talking under water.

"I'm sorry, Mr. Garfield isn't home right now. Can I help you? This is Mrs. Garfield."

Melanie's no longer at the table and as he speaks, Holden scans around. "—um, hello, Mrs. Garfield . . ." He can't see her anywhere. ". . . this is Mr. Garfield . . ." Finally spots her sitting with her back to him on the wooden sandbox. ". . . Mr. Garfield's son . . ." He cops a phrase from the sign on the wall in the restaurant. ". . . The Original," he adds.

"—oh my goodness is this Holden?"

She sounds nice.

Nice voice.

Warm.

"—yeah," he says.

Melanie has turned slightly sideways, leaning forward, talking to a little boy with pale blond hair playing with a plastic scoop shaped like a shovel in the sandbox.

"Well my goodness, Holden, this is Raine. It's so nice to finally talk to you! Your dad is going to be so disappointed that he's missed this call. Where are you? Give me your number so he can call you back . . ."

Melanie has charmed the little boy to come stand close to her and she's playing some kind of now-you-see-it-now-you-don't game that involves her touching the little boy's nose.

"—um, I'm calling from a pay phone, actually, but I can call again. I can call tomorrow, maybe, if that's good."

"—well, unfortunately, your father's at the summer White House with the President until the weekend, Holden . . ."

"—I didn't know there *was* a summer White House . . ."

She laughs low in her throat.

"—there isn't, but it sounds good, doesn't it?"

"—yeah . . . a little czarist, you know, winter palace, summer palace . . ."

He can tell she's warming to him.

"Congratulations, by the way, on . . . everything. The kid. The marriage . . ."

"—thank you."

"I hope the baby looks like you and not—" He almost says "Pooh" but stops himself in time.

She laughs again.

"Actually Peter says the baby looks like you," she says.

"How *is* . . . Peter?"

"Happy. In good shape. Happy with his work. Happy with his life . . ."

"—that's good," Holden says, letting that sink in. "That's important."

He lets his eyes embrace Melanie's form as she stands up. Somehow it never occurred to him before that his father and his mother might have been ill-suited for each other. Temperamentally. Physically. It just never occurred to him. That his father might have been unhappy, too, not only Kanga. He watches how the shape of Melanie's body, how her spine and hips show through his T-shirt when she leans over in the sandbox and picks up the little boy.

"—so what's the story with the two of you?" he asks.

She laughs again.

She's an easy laugher.

"—the 'story'?" she repeats.

Melanie slings her arms under the child's buttocks, teasing his legs around her waist, and bounces him a couple times before she kisses him.

"—the 'story' is we love each other up every chance we get," he hears her saying. "Holden?"

A couple women, one of them most certainly the young boy's mother, start to act alarmed by what they see is happening as Melanie steps out of the sandbox with the little boy held tightly to her and starts to walk away with him.

Adults from around the lawn start to move, first with tentative long steps, then slowly breaking into a run toward Melanie but Holden gets there first, positioning himself between her and the others, deftly swinging the little boy out of her arms through the air to place him firmly on the ground where he runs happily back to the spot in the sandbox where he left his shovel.

Her hand starts to move in fluid writing in the air as she stands absolutely still and watches him run off. Holden stares down the curious group until they're satisfied the child is safe, then he takes her by the arm and leads her to the van in silence.

DISILLUSIONMENT OCCURS only in the presence of illusion.

At its wake.

Or in its ruin.

Holden decides it's time to drive like a bat out of hell straight to Noah. Straight to her brother for help.

No more pissing around.

No more stops for the fun of it at the roadside attractions.

No more fucking whenever they want to for hours.

Driving ten hours with six hours off between shifts he can get them to the town where Noah lives in three days—four at the outside. Four days and three nights. From Corbin he sets a course straight west—due west, straight through Kentucky. Only that night she takes him like never before, with a gentle insistence that builds to abandon, straight as an arrow, from sweetness to frenzy through no diminuendo. And he knows he must sleep so he can get up and drive but he also knows he can no longer let her out of his sight.

"We'll be with Noah soon," he tells her that night, the gravid moon shedding silver light across their bodies through the windows of the van.

He props his head on his hand and surveys her, her nakedness. Her hand begins to move involuntarily across her belly, writing, and he clasps it, holding it still, but as soon as he lets go

she takes the movement up again. What are you writing, Johnnie?
he breathes, unaware that he's formed this thought aloud.

"—what?"

He studies her face, stills her hand again. If he let her write
against his back the way she first did in the hospital, if he let her
do that, and then if he wrote down her words, that would be one
way to reclaim her memory, he knows.

But there's another way, he thinks.

He could show her the notebooks.

He could start to read to her from them.

"Let me ask you something," he says, wondering which way
to go with this. "Do you remember ever keeping a diary?"

"—*me?* No."

"You never kept a diary or a journal. Wrote your thoughts
down in a notebook."

"—never. I'm terrible at writing. It takes me forever to collect my thoughts. Not like you . . ."

She sits up and props her back against the side of the van
opposite his and entwines her legs with his where they meet
across the bed.

"I wish you'd give me some of your articles to read," she says
casually.

"You're not missing anything, believe me, it's just news, just
straight reporting. There's nothing wonderful about it, you never
get to draw conclusions, it's endless facts in endless series . . ."

"Why did you quit?"

He wiggles his toes against hers for a while, then stares at her.
This is the first time she's ever really asked him about his world,
and although he wants to talk some more about the notebooks,
he decides to follow her in this direction.

"—you really want to know?" he says.

"—of course I do."

He thinks about it before telling her, "—come here, then. Over here." He doesn't want to have to look at her when he's talking about war, describing what he saw there. While he's telling her about the dead. About the day he saw the baby nailed to the tree. The only way that he can talk about it is by holding her, not looking in her eyes. Holding her, not letting her look into his. Not letting her see the thing he knows might still be there.

When he starts to talk it all comes back to him—finding people murdered in their houses, sitting at their tables with their spoons and forks still in their hands like they are still alive, the food congealed with maggots, the same maggots in the people's eyes. He tells her about the baby in the woods, and as he tells her, he finds, to his surprised relief, that he can allow himself to finally mourn, to weep for that dead baby, all the dead babies known and unknown of the earth including, though he cannot tell her this, her own. He tells her about the morning he came into Srebrenica—that killing field. He tells her that when he saw the evidence it held of slaughter, that mass genocide, instead of raging against the evil done upon that ground, his mind immediately went to the memory of his favorite image in fiction, the image of James Joyce's at the end of his story "The Dead" where he likens all the snow that's falling on the graveyards over Ireland, every differentiated nameless flake of snow to every individual nameless soul who's ever breathed a breath.

"And I felt ashamed."

Without his realizing it, at some moment in this long confession, they've shifted position. He's lying on his back, she's next to him, half on top of him, chin on his chest, face to face.

"—*why* did you feel ashamed?"

He runs his hand down her back.

"—for my selfishness. For trying to protect myself. For trying to numb the truth of what was in front of me by thinking about something so beautiful."

"You shouldn't feel ashamed of that," she says slowly. "Searching for something beautiful is what makes us divine. Some of us. What made you search for a beautiful thought in the face of such horror is the same reason we invent Heaven. The idea of beauty is the same as the idea of an ideal love—it promises healing. It stops the sorrow. Everyone needs a Heaven in them somewhere where they can go in their minds when everything—all of it—is lost."

Johnnie, kiss me he can barely whisper, and she does.

He runs his fingers through her hair, spreading it, like a halo, around her head.

"I wish I knew you," he murmurs.

"—but you do."

"In here," he says and cups her whole skull in his hands.

She smiles at him and for the first time love shows in her eyes.

"—thank you," he whispers, seeing it there. "I love you back."

He draws her head to his heart, slipping with ease into deep dreamless slumber.

It is the most deceiving thing.

At first you think it's just another ordinary thing on the horizon. A windmill, maybe. Radio transmitter. But its deception is: for a long long time it sits there.

You drive and drive and it just sits there never getting any larger.

Never getting closer, either. For fifty miles he had been watching it.

afraid of heights

Then all of a sudden it's on top of them and it's the biggest thing around.

"We have to see this," Holden says. "I know I said no more roadside attractions but this we gotta see . . . *this* is like the Bethlehem of the whole Civil War. Where the future Christ was born."

The weather had been dodgy all this morning, Kentucky Storm Watch K-Thirteen Ninety-nine reporting potential storms that never hatched, potential twisters that never touched the ground, in every county they had driven through—but they'd made great time across the state all the way from Corbin, the last fifty miles entirely dominated by this structure here in Fairview.

This monolith.

Erected, so the legend says, on the very spot where Jefferson Davis was born. The very spot, mind you.

"It says here," Melanie is reading from their Kentucky guidebook, "that it's only three hundred fifty-one feet tall. That's not very tall, as far as these things go. Why does it look so tall?"

"Because there's nothing else around," Holden tells her.

On the sidewalk in front of it there's a State Marker that reads, "Jefferson Davis Salute to Kentucky. Birthplace of the First and Only President of the Confederacy."

"'The Lost Cause,'" Holden muses, leaning back to try to see the top of it. "The 'First and Only.' And the irony is, if the South had won, Jeff Davis today would be less of a hero. We goin up?"

"—you bet!"

"You're not afraid of heights, are you?"

"We'll find out . . ."

When the elevator doors slide open you don't feel the impact right away because the elevator's in the perfect center of the

210

obelisk, but when you start toward the perimeter the whole three-sixty opens up.

"—*wow*," she murmurs.

"You okay?"

She nods but he can see that she's not at ease.

Her hand is on the move.

"You want to leave? We can go back down."

She shakes her head.

There are about thirty people up there with them, plus a couple State Park Rangers, and he can't tell whether it's the height or the crowd making her nervous so he puts an arm around her and draws her to the corner of the gallery with the fewest people.

And the view *is* magnificent.

"—which direction are we looking?"

"East—see?" He points. "The Blue Ridge Mountains where we were, over there. And there's the Cumberland—"

Suddenly a child's voice from the far side of the elevator cries out, "*Mommy!*" and Melanie reacts, her head turning toward the sound.

"*Mommy!* Over here!"

A human kind of buzzing noise arises from the side of the obelisk behind the elevator and Holden notices everybody turning from this side of the panorama toward the other. He reaches for Melanie's hand but another voice, another child's, calls, "*Mom!* You gotta come and see this! *Mom*, it's awesome!"

On that side the crowd is two abreast before the window.

And the light is very different.

A massive wall of ugly steel-grey cloud has taken over every inch of sky far off to the right on the distant horizon, like false night, or an invasion, and people in the front are given to expres-

tornado

sions of rapt awe. A little voice calls, *"Mom! Where are you?*
Come and look at this!" and Melanie pushes through.

A little late in piecing it together, as soon as Holden sees the
cloud he makes the silent prayer, "—oh god, just let it thunder.
Let it just be lightning, lord."

He's about a foot behind her when it happens, when the cir-
cuits in her brain switch back on, fizz and pop with startling news
like a new and powerful invention, and the first thing that she
does is turn her back on it and try to get to him but the memory
is *there*, it's already *there*, he can see its shape in her face and her
eyes. Her hands go up and the wail that pours forth out of her sets
people rushing for an exit, nervous, kids are crying, everybody
frightened of her, backing off with hands over their ears, their
faces contorted with panic and fear. "I'm here," he keeps saying,
"I'm here with you, darling," as he eases her down in his arms to
the floor and tells the Park Ranger who's drawn his gun to call an
ambulance, please. Within seconds there's no one at all with them
up there to share her grief and witness her wailing, and there's
nothing that Holden can do but keep saying, "I'm here" and
"You're not alone," as the sky way over there reaches its tentacle
down, its tornado to earth, with a deafening keening somewhere
that's equal to hers. Minutes go by, he looks out at the earth in
the foreground, at the land, at the farms and the houses and the
rooms and the beds and the framed photographs and the books
on the shelves and the boxes of letters and the scribbled poems of
youth and the diaries and the music that's sung in a voice you
remember, all these things, and more things you once knew but
have forgotten, and after a while somebody comes to inform him
The ambulance is downstairs, now, sir. And Holden asks if he'll
give them a little while longer, please, a minute or two to sit Up
Here in this towering monument to The Lost Cause and listen.

To the wind rushing by. To the wind rushing over the earth. A minute or two to get ready to take the next step and meet what Padge met every time he stepped into the sky.

The truth.

The awful truth that it's further and further from Heaven, all the way down.

ACKNOWLEDGMENTS
All weaknesses herein are mine; any glory is Ann Patty's.

Almost Heaven
A Novel

Marianne Wiggins

ABOUT THIS GUIDE

The suggested questions are intended to help your
reading group find new and interesting angles
and topics for discussion for Marianne Wiggins'
Almost Heaven. We hope that these ideas will enrich
your conversation and increase your
enjoyment of the book.

READING GROUP QUESTIONS AND TOPICS FOR DISCUSSION

1. Who is on Holden's list of "the ten men who have shaped his life"? What does the fact that he keeps a list like this tell us about Holden's character? What is he looking for, what does he value, and what about his current situation compels him to return to this list, searching for "grace, trust, and humility"? Why is his own father not on the list? Is Noah John his surrogate father?

2. Sleep-deprived in the Frankfurt airport, traumatized by his experiences, and possibly in the midst of a nervous breakdown, Holden contends with his memory's "flashbulb effect." What is the "flashbulb effect"? What is Holden remembering?

3. While Holden is lost in memories of his grandfather, Padge, his plane to Richmond is struck by lightning with the abruptness and mystery of a symphonic explosion, "like Beethoven composing." At this point, before any of the central plot of the novel has unfolded, Wiggins has already established two central themes, memory and weather. What connections exist between the two? How do these early scenes foreshadow how the story will unfold and eventually climax?

4. Consider the stark, almost poetic nature of the fragmented phrases and words at the top of each page of the novel. How do they add to the tone and themes of *Almost Heaven*? Which ones strike you the most? Why?

5. At one point Holden reflects on the way his own voice sounds, describing it as "willful" and "strident." Would you agree? Although Wiggins writes *Almost Heaven* in the third person, it is a third-person narrative that is filtered thoroughly and solely through Holden's perspective, and his voice seeps through every line of the novel. What narrative techniques and idiomatic structures does the author employ to portray Holden's often flip personality and ragged state of mind?

6. Is Holden's decision to take Melanie out of the hospital—ignoring Alex's advice and knowingly flirting with disaster—a selfish one? Is it noble? Why? What exactly are his motives? Why is the pursuit of a love that grows out of the absence of history and memory, a love that is utterly without baggage, so appealing to someone like Holden?

7. Is it possible that Holden's drive to shelter and preserve a woman's innocence—even a false and precarious innocence that hinges upon tragedy and amnesia—might be a doomed attempt to find an antidote to his haunted memories of the war in Bosnia? Explain. What other things might be motivating his actions?

8. Why do you suppose Wiggins chose the name Holden Garfield, with its strong echo of Holden Caulfield, the iconic protector of lost innocence in Salinger's *The Catcher in the Rye*? How are these two characters alike?

9. What happens to Melanie and Holden after the novel ends? In your reading group, construct a hypothetical extra chapter.

10. What is the significance of the title? Reread the single-page chapter that begins with "Somewhere there's a monument to the love that you haven't found yet." Why isn't the novel simply called *Heaven*?

11. In a novel concerned chiefly with the nature of memory and loss in the 1990s, what is Wiggins doing by punctuating Holden's journey with a relentless string of Civil War monuments and museums? Toward the end of *Almost Heaven*, Holden finally recognizes the utter emptiness in Melanie's eyes—"the Vacancy of meaning in a life whose history's been erased." At this point, what do we and Holden realize about the essence of the countless memorials that dot our landscape? Why is the presence of history, and of memory, so important?

12. In a powerhouse climax, Melanie's memory returns with the force of a tornado. Why is it so fitting that this happens—Melanie recovers her own personal tragedy, just as Holden loses sight of his own personal heaven—at the Jefferson Davis monument in Kentucky, the infamous site of The Lost Cause?